THE BABCOCK RANCH

MARY LEE PECK

ISBN: 9781797724454

Primary Publishing, Inc.
Westerville, Ohio

Babcock Ranch

Chapter 1

Jake Crowley stared at the fashionably dressed young woman stepping off the train onto the platform of the Billings, Montana depot. She looked out-of-place among the rough-looking miners and homesteaders piling off the smoke-belching, Northern Pacific train. Her pale blue traveling suit matched the bright blue of her eyes, and her raven hair heightened the paleness of her lily-white skin. She was so thin a slight chinook wind could easily send her rolling across the prairie like a bundle of blue tumbleweed.

Jake rolled his eyes upward. "Oh, please, Dear God, don't let her be Anna Babcock." He quickly scanned the other passengers hoping to see another twenty-something female stepping onto the platform, but none appeared. Most passengers had located their awaiting greeters and gaily engaged in hugs and animated conversations. Others raced toward the livery to get a horse to carry them to the prospecting fields and the promise of riches. Only the young woman in blue

Babcock Ranch

stood alone without anyone to welcome her. Her eyes met his, and she quickly looked away, apparently dismissing him as the person she was expecting.

Jake shook his head and apprehensively approached her. "I'm hoping I'm wrong, but you aren't Anna Babcock, are you?"

The young woman stiffened and looked up at the tanned, frowning face of the cowboy. His penetrating, dark-brown eyes glistened in the afternoon sun. "Yes. I am Anna Babcock. Who are you? I expected my grandmother's foreman Jake Crowley to meet me, and you are not him."

Jake lowered his head and scuffed his boot against the wide plank floor of the station platform. "My uncle Jake passed away a week after your grandmother died. I was named after him and have been working Mrs. Babcock's ranch for several years now. I am the only living and breathing Jake Crowley left in Montana as far as I know."

Anna straightened her posture and glared at Jake. "Well, it appears we are both disappointed in one another. Now, if you will direct me to the carriage, I would like to get to the ranch before dark."

Babcock Ranch

Jake chuckled. "Carriage?" He gently took her by the shoulders and slowly spun her around, carefully examining her apparel.

Anna forcefully shrugged his hands off. "Just what do you think you are you doing grabbing me that way, Mr. Crowley?"

Jake raised his eyebrows. "Well, our first stop will be at the Mercantile to get you some decent riding clothes." He glanced down at the huge trunk the Porter dropped off the wagon at her feet. "I don't suppose you have any riding clothing in there."

"No, I certainly do not. I did not need such apparel in New York?"

Jake exhaled a long, slow breath. He grabbed the trunk's leather handle and dragged it toward the small depot.

"Where are you taking my trunk?"

"We obviously can't carry this on horseback."

Anna froze in place. "Horseback?"

Jake said nothing.

She lifted her narrow skirt and scurried after him. "You don't honestly expect me to ride to the ranch on horseback, do you?"

Babcock Ranch

Jake whirled around and stared into her widened, condemning eyes. "You grew up on the ranch, did you not? According to your grandmother and my uncle, you were a good rider. So, I assume you can still ride. Besides, your grandmother has never owned a carriage, at least that I can remember." He let loose of the trunk allowing it to drop hard against the wooden planks and glared at her. "Can you or can you not ride a horse?"

Anna tugged on her short jacket and straightened her shoulders. "It's been years, but, yes, I once could ride quite well. Your uncle said I was a natural, but I haven't ridden since I left here five years ago to attend art school in New York."

"Well, we are about to find out just how much of a natural you are. Now, why don't you shuffle over to the Mercantile in those ridiculously, uncomfortable-looking satin shoes and buy yourself some riding clothes and boots?"

Anna drooped her chin to her chest and avoided eye contact with Jake. She felt the warmth on her cheeks from the blush spreading across her face. After a few seconds, she inhaled a quick breath and

Babcock Ranch

looked contritely up at him through her dark, curly eyelashes.

"Buy?" She slowly pulled against the drawstrings of her embroidered, satin pouch to open it and turned it upside down. "It's empty except for a lace-trimmed, linen handkerchief."

Jake stared at her with his eyes wide open and his mouth gaping. He yanked off his hat and ran his hand through his hair. "Do you mean you traveled across the country without any money?"

Anna fidgeted with the drawstrings on her purse. "I had only enough for my traveling clothes, my passage, and a few meals. Beginning artists don't typically earn a lot of money."

Jake glanced down at the huge trunk. "Well, perhaps you should have sold some of your clothes before you left New York. You won't have any use for fancy dresses and shoes out here."

Anna waved her hand toward the trunk. "It's mostly full of brushes, a few paintings, paint, and blank canvases; nothing of any value to anyone but me."

Jake stared at her for several seconds. Finally, her words reached his brain, and he shoved his hand into his pocket and pulled out a roll of

Babcock Ranch

bills. "Here!" He grabbed her hand and slapped the bills into her palm. "Now go over to the Mercantile and buy some boots and riding clothes."

"I'll pay you back, Jake. I promise—as soon as I sell the ranch." He grabbed her arm and leaned in close to her face. "Sell the ranch? You can't mean that. Do you have any idea of the hardships your grandparents and parents endured getting and preserving that ranch for you? They are buried on Babcock Ranch for God's Sakes." He squeezed her arm tighter. "They must be spinning in their graves right now."

Anna jerked her arm loose and backed away from him. She stared down at her uncomfortable shoes for several seconds before slowly raising her eyes to meet his. "Of course, I know how my parents and grandparents struggled out here. I saw my grandfather and my father die from wounds in skirmishes with bands of rogue Indians. My mother died giving birth to me because no one was there to help her the day I was born. But, Jake, look at me. Be honest. You knew the moment you saw me I wasn't what you expected. I have neither the

Babcock Ranch

skill nor the inclination to run a ranch—nor do I have the will and

fortitude my parents and my grandparents had to survive out here.

My life is in New York. I am not my grandmother."

She stormed away toward the exit leading to the main street of

Billings. Without having to look back, she felt the anger burning

through her jacket that was no doubt flashing in Jake's dark, irate

eyes.

Babcock Ranch

Chapter 2

When she reached the end of the path leading up a small incline to town, Anna stopped and stared in awe at the tremendous changes to the small prairie town she once knew. When she had left for New York, the possibility of a train reaching Billings was just a dream in the minds of a small number of ranchers like her grandmother who had learned to coexist with the Sioux and Cheyenne tribes controlling most of the territory.

"My goodness, this doesn't look at all like the Billings I once knew." She carefully crossed the deep-rutted, dirt street and headed toward the Mercantile. Stopping at the bottom of the wooden steps leading to its entrance, she stared up at the expansive, sturdy-looking building. It was at least three times the size it used to be. When she had left Billings, the Mercantile served as the post office, hardware, and general store. It was not much more than a clapboard shanty with a tin roof that threatened to blow away in even the slightest gust

Babcock Ranch

of wind. Only a few other buildings were part of the small town back then—mostly saloons.

She glanced up and down the main street at the long row of permanent-looking establishments. "My, what a difference five years makes."

"Even a month changes things around here." Colonel Robert Holloway removed his large, brimmed hat and bowed at the waist. "Welcome to Billings. Colonel Holloway at your service."

Anna nodded and quickly curtsied. "I'm sorry. I didn't know anyone was within earshot of me." She offered her hand to the Colonel. "I'm Anna Babcock. I just arrived on the train after having been gone for five years. I am amazed at how different the town is."

"Ah, so you are Anna Babcock. I have heard of your grace and beauty, but I must say the rumors fell considerably short of accurately describing you. I noticed you walking from the train station. You stand out from the regulars in Billings by extreme measure."

Babcock Ranch

Anna felt a warmth rush to her cheeks. She lowered her eyes and didn't respond.

Colonel Holloway smiled. "I'm sorry. I can see I have embarrassed you. That wasn't my intention. May I ask if you need transportation out to your grandmother's ranch?"

"You knew my grandmother?"

"Yes. Everyone knew her or at least knew of her. She is, or was, part of the tapestry of Billings." He took Anna's hand again and lightly patted it. "I am sorry not only for your loss but for all of Billings. Her passing affected all of us."

"Thank you, Colonel. As to your question about transportation to the ranch, my grandmother's foreman, Jake Crowley, has arranged to escort me back to the ranch on horseback. Thus, my trip to the Mercantile." She held out the side of her skirt. "I'm afraid I was unprepared for such a means of transportation. I can't very well ride horseback in this outfit now, can I."

Babcock Ranch

The Colonel smiled and nodded. "No, you could not. I'm surprised Jake didn't think ahead to provide a lady like yourself a more suitable means of transportation."

"I guess he thought I would be more … well, I'm not sure what he thought, but if you'll excuse me, I need to purchase some more suitable riding clothes." She started up the plank steps.

Colonel Holloway lightly touched her elbow to assist her. "I would be honored if you would let me carry you out to your ranch. I stable my horses and carriage in the livery across the street. It will just take a few minutes for me to retrieve them."

For the first time, Anna looked directly at the Colonel. He was quite handsome. Light streaks of gray highlighted his dark, wavy hair at the temples. A small scar on his cheek was the only defect on his perfectly featured face. His eyes were deep-set and dark and his posture confident, but something about him made her uneasy. As an artist, she was trained to see beyond outward appearances and look for the feelings reflected in a person's eyes, posture, and smile.

Babcock Ranch

Colonel Holloway had a broad smile, but it seemed forced and never reached his eyes, which remained dark and menacing.

"I wouldn't want to trouble you, Colonel. I am perfectly capable of riding. I am looking forward to it after being away from the ranch for so long." She glanced across the street and saw Jake walking the two horses toward them. "Oh, I see Jake heading this way now. I really must go inside so I won't hold him up. We want to get to the ranch before dark. Thanks for your kind offer. Perhaps, we can take a carriage ride another time." She quickly climbed the steps to the Mercantile.

"I will make sure of it," the Colonel called after her.

The tone of his voice caused a chill to run through her, and she quickened her steps.

The young woman behind the counter looked up as Anna burst through the door. "Good afternoon, Miss. Are you all right? You are flushed."

Anna drew in a deep breath. "I'm fine. Thanks for asking. I ran up the stairs too quickly because I am in rather a hurry."

Babcock Ranch

The young woman stared at Anna for several seconds. "Anna Babcock? Is it actually you?" She rushed out from behind the counter and grabbed Anna's hands spreading them apart so she could see her entire silhouette. "It is you. You are thinner, but I would recognize that dark hair and those deep violet eyes anywhere."

A smile spread across Anna's face. "Courtney Livingston!" She grabbed Courtney and hugged her tight. "Thank goodness! What a relief to see someone I recognize."

Courtney squealed with delight. "I have missed you more than you will ever know. The last time I saw you, tears streamed down your cheeks as you climbed into that rickety ol' stagecoach headed for New York." Her smile suddenly disappeared, and she hugged Anna. "I am so sorry about your grandmother, Sweetie." She held Anna for several seconds before letting her go.

Anna drew in a deep breath. "When I heard she was sick, I tried to scrape enough money together to get here, but I couldn't come up with it soon enough. She didn't want me to come and kept insisting she was fine. You know how she was—never taking things seriously

Babcock Ranch

and always believing things would work themselves out." She reached into her pouch and pulled out the handkerchief to stop the tears building up in her eyes from flowing down her cheeks.

Courtney gave her another quick hug. "Well, you're here now, and I couldn't be happier. Hey, what do you think of my store?"

"Your store?"

"Yes. I bought it several years ago and recently expanded it. Well, it's not all mine, yet. Colonel Holloway financed it for me."

Anna looked around at the large shopping space and the variety of merchandise stacked on tall shelves and displayed on flat tables and inside glass front display cases. "It's amazing. I'm impressed, but what do you mean Colonel Holloway financed it for you?"

"He loaned me the money, and I make a monthly loan payment. His interest charges are higher than the bank's, but the bank wouldn't loan me the money at all. George Murphy, president of the First National Bank, politely told me women are a business risk."

Anna decided not to share her concerns about Colonel Holloway; not right now, anyway.

Babcock Ranch

"Of course, I don't carry the fashionable suits like you are wearing, but I bet you could use some more practical clothes for the ranch, right?"

Anna chuckled. "Absolutely. I need some riding clothes right away. Jake Crowley met me at the train with two horses. He's waiting for me outside, so I need to grab something fast."

"Jake met you, huh? So, what do you think of him? He's as good looking as they come, don't you think?"

Anna wrinkled her nose. "I didn't notice."

Courtney burst out laughing. "I don't believe for a minute you didn't notice how handsome he is. Those dark brown eyes of his send shivers to my core and his smile makes my heart skip a beat."

Anna shrugged. "I have only seen him frown and scowl. He's rather overbearing and irritable if you ask me."

"He's probably afraid you just came here to sell your grandmother's ranch."

Anna flinched and looked down at the floor.

Babcock Ranch

Courtney drew in a quick breath. "Oh no. You wouldn't do that; would you?"

Anna slowly shrugged. "I don't know, Courtney. My life is in New York. I left here because I knew I could never run the ranch."

Courtney put her hands on her hips. "No. You are wrong. You left here because your grandmother made you leave. You begged her to let you stay. She wanted you to get a good education and explore other opportunities, but she always knew you would find your way back here. She never once doubted you'd come back to stay."

Anna stared at Courtney for several seconds. "How do you know that?"

"She told me. Every time she picked up a letter from you, she'd read it to me. After she'd read it, she folded it up and put it back in the envelope. Then she'd look at me and flash that ornery grin of hers and say, 'She's getting closer to coming home. Won't be long now.' I don't know what it was in your letters that led her to think you'd be coming home, but she said it every time."

Babcock Ranch

"Strange. I never once mentioned coming home. Anyway, I can't afford to keep the ranch if it isn't self-supporting, which as I recall it rarely was. I am truly a starving artist."

"I can't wait to see some of your paintings. You should display them in here. As Billings expands, wealthier people are moving in. They are always looking for decorating items for their lavish homes. Wait 'til you see the Moss Mansion. It's huge."

"I've read about in New York. The architect also designed the luxurious Waldorf Astoria."

Jake burst through the door of the Mercantile. He glared at Anna. "I thought you wanted to get to the ranch before dark?"

Courtney frowned at him. "For Pete's Sake, Jake. Is that any way to speak to your boss and my long-lost friend?"

"Sorry Jake, I was just catching up with Courtney." She quickly grabbed a pair of brown leather gauntlets and boots from a table display and a split riding skirt and a white bodice from a round rack.

"You can change behind the dressing screen in the back, Anna." As Anna rushed toward the back of the store, Courtney glared at Jake.

Babcock Ranch

"What's put a burr in your breeches, Jake? I've never seen you treat anyone so rudely."

Jake shook his head. "She only came back here to sell the ranch. You saw her. She doesn't fit in here."

"Well, she used to fit in, and she loved this town and the ranch."

"That's hard to believe. From what I heard from her, she intends to head back to New York as fast as she can."

Courtney laid her hand on Jake's shoulder. "Instead of trying to drive her off, maybe you should turn on that charm of yours and convince her to stay."

"I don't play games, Courtney."

Courtney cocked her head to the side. "Well, maybe you should."

Chapter 3

The sunlight poured in through her bedroom window at the ranch and awakened Anna. She stretched her arms above her head and rubbed her eyes. A smile spread across her face as she stared out at the picturesque view of the tip of the sun peeking above the mountains in the distance and sending bright rays of yellow and orange across the morning sky. A childhood memory flashed through her mind of her grandmother's feisty rooster loudly announcing the beginning of every new day. When she was young, she loved to snuggle down under the thick covers to watch the sunrise each morning. She had forgotten how beautiful Montana mornings were. The sun warmed her face and brightened the room with a cheerful, yellow glow.

She pulled the heavy, hand-sewn quilt up tighter under her chin and sighed. Her smile slowly faded as she thought about Jake Crowley and his vehement objection to her decision to sell the ranch. She flopped over and covered her head with a pillow.

Babcock Ranch

"I don't have a choice." Her voice bounced off the log walls of the huge bedroom. She lay motionless for several minutes before finally tossing off the quilt and sitting up on the side of the bed. "No sense wallowing in self-pity. I have horses and other animals to feed, eggs to gather, and goats to milk." She glanced over at her grandmother's picture staring across the room at her from atop the crocheted runner on the maple dresser. Her grandmother's broad smile radiated joy and self-assuredness. Anna slowly walked over and picked up the photo. Lightly touching the familiar face, she sighed. "I'm truly sorry I can't be you, Granny. But times have changed, and so have I."

A loud thud on the front porch made her jump. "What was that, for heaven's sake?"

 She grabbed her grandmother's housecoat and headed into the large, open space of the house serving as the living, kitchen, and dining rooms. Opening the front door, she saw Jake pulling away with a team of horses harnessed to a large, wooden wagon. He didn't look her way. In fact, he hadn't looked at or spoken to her since they had

Babcock Ranch

left the Mercantile yesterday. On the ride to the ranch from town, he rode in front of her the entire way and never once looked back to see if she was following him. Thank goodness, she could stay on the horse without much difficulty. By the time they reached the ranch, she sat straight in the saddle and moved easily to the horses' smooth gallop. She was proud she hadn't forgotten how to ride and surprised at how much she enjoyed it.

She reached down and grabbed the leather handle on her trunk which Jake tossed onto the porch. With all the strength she could muster, she dragged it across the wooden plank floor into the house. He had evidently picked it up at the station last night or perhaps early this morning. She was surprised he bothered to bring it to the ranch at all. That he didn't care for her was unmistakably evident.

Suddenly ravenous, she rummaged through the kitchen cupboards. A broad grin spread across her face. "I won't have to shop for food for weeks, which, given my current lack of funds, is a godsend. I could feed most of Billings with this amount of food. I wonder if I have Jake to thank for all this, or if it is the remnants of Granny's

Babcock Ranch

tendency to keep a huge stock of food because she hated going into town. Either way, I am grateful."

After a quick breakfast, she slipped into a flowered gingham dress she found in her bedroom closet. Granny must have expected her to come home. Everything in her bedroom was just as she had left it when she went to New York, including the small wardrobe she had left behind.

Quickly glancing at herself in the large, antique floor mirror, she scowled and turned from side-to-side. "I guess I have lost some weight since I left." She sighed and glanced upward. "I missed your great cooking every day while I was in New York, Granny, and I missed you, too. Oh, how I wish you were here now." She brushed away a single tear and drew in a deep breath. "Well, tears are not going to bring you back." She headed toward the bedroom door. "Here goes day one of what I intend to be a very short stint at ranch work."

Heading outside, she stopped at the gate leading into the chicken coop. A basket full of fresh eggs sat outside the hen house atop a

Babcock Ranch

wooden crate. She felt the eggs. The shells were still slightly soft and warm. Someone already gathered the morning eggs.

When she entered the barn, a pale of fresh goat's milk sat by the door, and the animals in the barn munched on grain and fresh hay. The stalls and pens were clean and full of fresh straw and clean water. She looked around the barn. Everything was organized and neat. "Now what am I supposed to do for the rest of the day?"

Jake led his horse out of one of the stalls. "You can go back to the house and get started on cooking dinner. We will be riding back here about 6:00 tonight and will expect to eat shortly after."

At the sound of Jake's demanding tone, Anna whirled around ready for an argument. "Oh, so you're finally going to talk to me, are you?" She put her hands on her hips and glared at him. "Well, I'll have you know I am not about to cook for a bunch of dust-covered ranch hands."

Jake tightened the girth of his saddle and flashed her a taunting grin. "I'm guessing you can't cook, right?"

Babcock Ranch

Anna stomped her foot and dug her hands deeper into her side. "No, you are wrong. I am a good cook. I had that in common with my grandmother."

"Good. Now's your chance to prove you can be useful around here." Anna glared at him. "Do you seriously expect me to cook three meals a day for you and the ranch hands? I don't recall my grandmother ever doing such a thing. A cook rode out on the range with her and the other ranch hands."

Jake shrugged. "That was then, and this is now. To make it simple for you, the ranch can't afford to hire a cook. I've been doing the cooking since Miss Babcock passed, but since you're here, I won't have to." He swung himself into the saddle. "As I said, we'll be back around six. I fixed breakfast in the bunkhouse this morning and sent some dry rations with the others for lunch. But from now on, I will turn the cooking, egg gathering, stall cleaning, feeding and milking over to you. I wouldn't want you to feel as if there was nothing for you to do around here. Your grandmother's recipes are in the tin box

Babcock Ranch

above the stove." He tipped his hat and spurred his horse into a full gallop without looking back.

Anna could still hear him laughing long after she could no longer see him. She stomped her foot and glared toward the cloud of dust in the distance. "You have got to be kidding me. I do not intend to cook three meals a day for a bunch of rowdy ranch hands." She trudged out of the barn and headed toward the house. Suddenly aware of a sound behind her, she abruptly stopped. Something or someone was following her. Her unrestrained imagination instantly seized control of her brain. Still aware the peace made with local Indians was somewhat fragile and bears, wolves, and other wild animals were very much a part of the natural habitat surrounding the ranch, she whirled around expecting to encounter a dangerous intruder. The rapid beating of her heart suddenly stalled as her eyes located the perpetrator. Relieved to discover her stalker was a friendly-looking yellow dog, she knelt and held her trembling hand out to him. "Who are you, fella?"

Babcock Ranch

The dog sat back on its haunches and softly whined. Mud and burrs covered him from head to tail, and dried blood crusted over a deep cut on his right foreleg.

"You poor, little guy. You look like you've had a rough time of it, and I bet you haven't eaten in a while." She lightly stroked him on the head. "Why don't you come with me and let me help you." Standing up, she patted her thighs and made soft kissing sounds with her lips to get the dog to follow her.

The dog simply cocked his head from side to side and stared at her through dark, sad eyes.

"Come on fella." She pointed to the house. "I have food for you in the house, but you'll have to come with me."

The yellow dog stretched out on the ground and rested his head on his sore paw. He rolled his eyes up at her and whimpered.

Anna pursed her lips and frowned. "Well, I can't carry you. You're much too big for me to try that." She slowly walked toward the house, glancing over her shoulder to see if the dog would follow her, but he didn't. She stopped and put her hands on her hips. "Well,

Babcock Ranch

aren't you the stubborn one—just like another male I have recently met. Fine, then. Wait there, and I will be right back."

She rushed into the house and grabbed a can of sausages from a kitchen shelf. Quickly prying the can open with a knife and grabbing a clean dishcloth from a drawer, she headed back outside. The dog hadn't moved from the spot where she had left him.

"Here you are fellow." She dumped the sausages on the ground in front of him and hurried over to the pump to wet down the cloth. When she returned, the sausages were gone. "You must have inhaled them. I've never seen so many sausages disappear so fast." Getting down on her knees, she gently wiped the dried blood from the cut. "Wow, the cut is deep. I bet you got tangled up with some barbed wire."

Remembering her grandmother always kept some antiseptic powder in the barn to treat injured animals, she jumped up and ran toward the main barn. Without hesitation, she went straight to the storage cabinet where they had always kept the first-aid kit. She smiled as

Babcock Ranch

she reached in and pulled out the familiar metal box. "Some things just never change."

Turning around quickly, she almost stepped on the big, yellow dog. "Well, you decided to follow me, did you? First, I think we'd better do something about those burrs and mud."

Plopping down on a bale of hay, she began to carefully remove the burrs from the poor dog's short fur. She then washed him down with some lye soap in a large steel tub outside. He was patient and often lovingly licked her hand. Finally, she gently lifted his injured paw and, taking the small scissors from the box, she began trimming away the fur around the cut before sprinkling the powder into the wound.

"This won't hurt a bit, but you mustn't lick it off." She smiled. How many times had she heard her grandmother say those words? She carefully wrapped the wound with some strips of torn cloth she found in the metal box. "There. That should do the trick."

She stood up and looked down at her dress. Brown stains and burrs covered the skirt. "I look as bad as you did a while ago."

Babcock Ranch

From outside, she heard the pounding of horses' hooves and the rattling of a carriage. A shadow fell on the ground in front of the open barn door, and the yellow dog immediately jumped in front of her. The hackles on the back of his neck raised, and he made a low, guttural growl. Anna raised her hand to shade her eyes to get a better look at the man now standing in the doorway.

"Colonel Holloway, what are you doing here?" She reached down and patted the dog. "It's all right, fella."

"You have quite a protective watchdog there, Miss Babcock."

"Yes, it would seem so." She blew upward through her lower lip to move a strand of her hair that fell over her eye and attempted to brush off the dog hair and burrs clinging to her skirt. "I apologize for my appearance, Colonel, but I wasn't expecting any company out here."

She glanced over at him and immediately felt uncomfortable about the way he was looking at her. She reached down to touch the dog. "What is it you want, Colonel Holloway?"

"I came to take you on that carriage ride I promised you."

Babcock Ranch

Anna looked away from his menacing eyes and pretended to be engrossed in rearranging the things in the metal box. "I apologize, Colonel Holloway, but I have too much to do before the ranch hands come back for dinner." She was immediately sorry she had admitted she was alone on the ranch. Slowly closing the metal box, she cast a brief look at him. "I am sorry you made the long trip out here for nothing."

The Colonel cleared his throat and slowly twirled his hat around in his hand. "I am not accustomed to having a young woman refuse my offer for an afternoon carriage ride, Miss Babcock. I have, after all, made a considerable effort to grant you your wish for a second chance to ride with me. Perhaps, you would care to reconsider your quick response."

Anna glared at him. A hot blush rushed to her face. "No sir, I do not. Now, if you will excuse me, I have some work to do up at the house." She started toward the door, but Colonel Holloway moved in front of her blocking her exit.

Babcock Ranch

"If it is your appearance you are concerned about, Miss Babcock, I will be glad to wait for you to change into that lovely suit you were wearing yesterday. A beautiful woman such as yourself should not be expected to wear gingham and muck around in a barn. Please, allow me to treat you the way you deserve."

When he reached for her hand, the yellow dog instantly charged at him pouncing against his chest and sending him flying backward. He stumbled against the tub Anna had used to bathe the dog and barely avoided falling into the dirty water. After regaining his balance, he dug his boot into the dog's side and sent him flying through the air. The poor animal howled in pain.

Anna ran to him and knelt beside him. She glowered at the Colonel. "You didn't have to kick him. He thought I was in danger and was protecting me."

The Colonel picked up his hat and slapped it against his leg. "Dog's need to learn respect, Miss Babcock. If they are allowed to be ruled solely by their instincts rather than by human commands, they are of no use and should be destroyed."

Babcock Ranch

Anna's face burned as anger rushed through her body. "I admire the power of animal's instincts, Colonel. I particularly respect the insightfulness of horses and dogs. I have always found them to be instinctively good judges of character and keenly aware of potential threats. I will thank you to be on your way, Colonel. Good day, sir." She walked briskly toward the house with the dog close by her side. Once inside, she dropped down and buried her face in the dog's fur. "Thank you, fella. I am so sorry he hurt you." Gently pushing against his side where the Colonel had kicked him, she watched the dog closely to see if he flinched indicating he might have suffered an internal injury. Relieved he appeared to be all right, she cupped her hands around his wide jowls and stared deeply into his dark eyes. "You were correct in your judgment of that man. He is dangerous." Slowly getting up and moving to the kitchen window, she watched as a cloud of dust from the Colonel's racing carriage hovered in the air. She had angered a very powerful man. "I hope I don't regret my treatment of him. I am certain he has the resources to destroy anyone who doesn't acquiesce to his commands."

Babcock Ranch

Chapter 4

Robert Holloway stormed into his office ignoring the nauseatingly cheerful greeting of Miss Collier, his Secretary. At that moment, he could have gladly choked her. No one had the right to be that happy when he was so miserable. He slammed the door of his private office and slung his hat across the room.

"Dammit it!" He paced back and forth in front of his huge walnut desk and slammed his fist against the front of it each time he passed by. "How dare the haughty Miss Babcock order me off her property. Doesn't she know I could squash her like an annoying mosquito anytime I chose to do so?"

He unfastened his gun belt and tossed it onto the red velvet divan. Closing his eyes, he slowly shook his head back and forth. Unfortunately, I can't get her out of my mind. The moment I saw her in front of the Mercantile, she stirred a deep yearning in me I can't ignore. I will soon acquire the Babcock Ranch when it comes up for auction in two weeks. That will make me the largest property owner

Babcock Ranch

in Yellowstone County, but that's no longer enough. I want the beautiful Anna Babcock and her ranch.

"That stupid dog ruined everything." He kicked the brass waste can and sent it sailing across the room scattering its contents everywhere. "No, I did."

He plopped down in his leather desk chair and whirled around to stare out the large window at the mountains. The view typically calmed him but not today. Again, his inability to control his anger produced disappointing results. When would he learn? Why couldn't he control his angry impulses? He closed his eyes and inhaled a long, slow breath. He knew precisely why he was so quick to strike out at anything or anyone who dared to disobey him. He had learned it from his father. His father struck first then asked questions or listened to reason later. Daily beatings with whatever his father could grab were routine for him growing up. But now he was an adult, and he understood his anger was misguided. He was still fighting his father, not the object or person in front of him.

"If I know this, why can't I control my anger?"

Babcock Ranch

In the military, his outbursts had kept him from a desired promotion. In his business life, he had lost deals because he was impatient and demeaning to potential partners or clients. He slammed his fist in his hand. "I saw how Anna Babcock looked at me—distrust and fear shone in her eyes."

Miss Collier's timid knock on his door interrupted his thoughts.

"What do you want?"

"I'm sorry, Colonel Holloway, but Tom Jacobs is here to see you."

"Send him away."

"But you asked me to have him meet with you this afternoon."

Colonel Holloway didn't respond, but the continued sound of muffled voices in the outer office irritated him. He jumped up and shoved his chair out of his way. It slid across the room, crashing against his large floor safe and finally tipping over. He stormed across the room and yanked open the door.

Miss Collier and Tom Jacobs jumped back and whirled around to face him.

Babcock Ranch

Miss Collier opened her mouth to speak, but his warning glare sent her quickly retreating behind her desk. He was in one of his moods, and she knew he was dangerous during such times. Poor Tom.

Colonel Holloway grabbed Tom by the arm and dragged him into his office.

Once inside, Tom nervously twisted his hat around in his hands while the Colonel picked up the chair and dragged it back to his desk. "You wanted to see me, Colonel?"

Holloway drew in a deep breath. "Yes, I did. I want to know why you and the others have not yet captured that wild stallion that has been stealing away my mares."

"I figured you'd be wanting to talk to me about that. We have chased that fool horse half-way across the territory, but every time we get close enough to throw a rope on him, he charges toward us and frightens our horses so bad that they take off in the opposite direction."

Babcock Ranch

"Then shoot him. I don't care if he is captured dead or alive. I want him to stop raiding my herd. You can certainly understand that, can't you?"

Tom nodded. "Sure, but It would be a shame to kill such a majestic animal. I thought you wanted to break him for racing."

"I've changed my mind. He's not worth saving. He probably could never be broke anyway."

Tom opened his mouth to argue but thought better of it. "I am glad to report we've been able to cause Crowley and his men some trouble keeping the Babcock steers rounded up. We've driven off at least 50 and are holding them in the northern canyon where they're not likely to be found."

"Only 50? Such a small number isn't likely to bankrupt the Babcock Ranch. What the hell are you thinking?"

Tom looked down at the floor. "That Indian working for Jake Crowley is sly as a fox, and it won't be long 'till he catches us cutting the fence."

Babcock Ranch

Colonel Holloway shrugged and let out a long, exasperated sigh.

"You carry a gun. Use it."

Tom's eyes opened wide. "You want me to kill him?"

Colonel Holloway walked around from behind his desk and grabbed Tom by the front of his shirt. "You either follow my instructions, or I will replace you with someone who will. And, of course, you know too much about me, so I can't simply let you leave. I intend to win the election for State Senator next time around, and I can't afford to have someone like you shooting off your mouth about how I do things. Understand?"

Beads of sweat gathered on Tom's forehead and ran down his face. He swallowed hard and nodded. "Yes, sir. I understand all right."

Babcock Ranch

Chapter 5

Anna spent the remainder of the morning unpacking her trunk and setting up a studio next to the large picture window in what used to serve as Granny's private parlor. She felt closer to her grandmother in that part of the house. The natural lighting from the window was perfect, and the view of the mountains in the background would inspire. She carefully unwrapped the brown paper from the four paintings that were to have been a gift for Granny's seventieth birthday. She lined them up side-by-side. She was proud of them and considered them her best work. Last year she entered them in the New York Winter Art Show and won first prize. Although she had many proposals from collectors and dealers to purchase or display them, she refused all offers. Art critics described the paintings as "the artist's beautiful depiction of a spiritual fantasy," but she knew the scene was not a figment of her imagination. The girl and the horse gliding across the moonlit pasture in the shadow of the

Babcock Ranch

mountains were real. She was the girl, and the horse was her beautiful, sorrel stallion, Luna.

She glanced out at the mountains. "I wonder if I will ever see him again." She sighed and looked down at the yellow dog. The look of despair in his eyes surprised her. He softly whimpered and lay down on the floor next to the paintings. She sat down on the floor next to him and rested her arm lightly on his back. "Why so sad, fellow? Do you know my horse?" She shook her head and chuckled at the silliness of her suggestion.

"You know what you need is a name. I can't go around calling you 'fella' all the time." Drawing her knees to her chest beneath her full skirt, she wrapped her arms around them and slowly rocked back and forth as she considered random names that flashed through her mind. Finally, she lifted the dog's head to rest it in her lap. "How would you like to be called Maximus? It means 'the greatest'."

The dog raised his head, barked, and thumped his long tail against the wooden floor.

Babcock Ranch

Anna laughed and bent over to lightly kiss the bridge of his nose.

"Well, then, Maximus, why don't I get these pictures placed on the mantle above the fireplace, and then I'll fix us some lunch."

As she sat at the oilcloth-covered table munching on a piece of cheese and a slice of somewhat stale sourdough bread, she thumbed through the tin box of recipes. Her grandmother's fingerprints stained every card. She fought hard to hold back tears as she recalled the countless meals she had helped Granny prepare and share with friends, ranch hands, and even strangers. Granny invited any visitor who wandered onto the ranch to stay for a meal. She rolled her eyes as a momentary twinge of guilt about her treatment of Colonel Holloway this morning flashed through her mind. She shook her head and sat up straighter. My situation was different. I am a young, unmarried female, and I am confident entertaining a male guest alone would be frowned on; even in New York. Besides, I don't care for him and do not want to give him any encouragement to pursue a relationship with me.

Babcock Ranch

She pulled out a well-stained recipe. "Shepherd's Pie. I haven't had that for years." She quickly read aloud the list of ingredients. "Ground beef, butter, onion, potatoes, corn, garlic, and seasonings." She flipped the card over hoping for instructions, but the backside of the card was blank. "Of course, it would be. Granny never measured anything and used whatever seasonings she had available or felt like using."

Wrinkling her forehead and tightly squinting her eyes, she tried to picture in her mind how to make the popular dish. She recalled the beef, garlic, and onions were browned and smothered with gravy. Then, they were covered with corn and mashed potatoes with the potatoes on top. The whole skillet was placed in the oven and baked. But, at what temperature? For how long?

She slumped back in the straight-back chair. Maybe I should stick with something I know how to fix—beef roast, mashed potatoes, corn, and biscuits. "This meal has to be delicious Maximus, or I will never live it down."

Babcock Ranch

Rummaging through the smokehouse, she found a large roast soaking in a barrel of salt brine. She held her breath as she struggled to lift the meat from the reeking brine. The roast was heavier than she anticipated, and once she had wrestled it from the barrel, it slipped through her hands and almost dropped onto the dirt floor. Raising one leg and precariously balancing the roast on her knee, she struggled to slide the wooden lid back on top of the barrel. She finally managed to get both arms wrapped around the slippery roast and headed for the door.

"This would be a whole lot easier in New York, Maximus. I would simply call the local butcher, tell him how many people I intended to serve, and how I planned to serve the meat. Later, I would walk two blocks and pick up a roast neatly wrapped in brown paper and waiting for me to arrive." She heaved a long sigh. "Come on, Maximus. I have something I need to prove to Mr. Jake Crowley."

Promptly at 6:00, a knock on her door announced the arrival of the ranch hands. She quickly glanced at the table and ran her hands

Babcock Ranch

down her clean apron to smooth it against one of her favorite dresses she had found in her closet.

On the table, she replaced the oilcloth with one of Granny's white linen tablecloths and used the good dinnerware and glass tumblers full of water she had cooled in the herb cellar. She carefully arranged a bouquet of marigolds and daisies in a crystal vase and placed it in the center of the table. She inhaled a long deep breath. "Hopefully, this will impress the doubting Jake Crowley."

When she opened the door, the neat appearance of the ranch hands surprised her. Each wore a fresh, white shirt tucked into clean jeans and were clean-shaven with their hair neatly combed. They certainly did not look like the ranch hands she had anticipated or that she had remembered from her childhood. Jake was intentionally trying to prove something to her too.

"Good evening, Gentlemen. Please come in." As they filed past her, the eldest of them was the last to enter. She instantly recognized him and threw both arms around his neck. "Avonaco! You are still here."

Babcock Ranch

The elderly Indian smiled broadly and gently patted her on the back. "Yes, little Archisa. I am still here and quite pleased you have returned. I have missed our long talks. Things will be better now that you have found your way home."

Anna glanced over at Jake and was not surprised to see the anger in his eyes. He had evidently not told the others of her plan to sell the ranch. She lightly touched Avonaco's arm. "No one has called me Archisa since I left here."

Avonaco smiled. "You remember that Archisa means 'ray of light' in Cheyenne. If you don't mind, I will continue to call you Archisa since you are indeed a ray of light to all of us. Darkness fell on this ranch after you left us, so I am glad you have brought back the light."

A deep pang of guilt caused her to avoid further eye contact with Avonaco.

Maximus paddled over and plopped down in front of Jake, who immediately squatted down and roughly rubbed and patted him. "Who is this?"

Babcock Ranch

"His name is Maximus—or at least that is the name I have assigned to him."

"The greatest, huh?"

It surprised her that Jake understood the meaning of his name. "He just showed up this morning after you left. He had a deep cut on his right foreleg. I cleaned him up, and he stayed."

Jake looked up at her. "You cleaned him up?"

Anna's cheeks burned. "Yes. I removed all the burrs from his coat, bathed him, and cleaned out his wound. Why do you find that so incredulous?"

Jake shrugged.

Avonaco noticed the paintings and walked over to the fireplace. He carefully studied each one. Anna approached him and linked her arm with his. "Do you like them? I painted them for Granny, but she was gone before I could send them to her."

With a hint of tears glistening in his eyes, Avonaco smiled at her.

"She would have loved them. They are beautiful. You have beautifully portrayed each phase of your dance with him."

Babcock Ranch

Anna looked at him with intense yearning. "Have you seen him? Does he still come here?"

Avonaco shook his head. "Not since the day you left. Even though he has never returned, it will be a full moon tonight. Maybe he will come back to you."

Jake moved in closer to the paintings. "I know that horse. I have seen him standing on the edge of the mountain overlooking our grazing land. The ranchers around here despise him. He raids their herds and runs off with their best mares. Colonel Holloway's men have been tracking him for weeks. Holloway has offered a substantial award for his capture, dead or alive."

Anna gasped and tightened her hold on Avonaco's strong arm. He patted her hand. "It is in the Hands of the Great Father, my little Archisa. He will protect him."

Jake watched her response. "I suppose you have a fantasy of someday taming him and riding him across the pasture like the images in your paintings. You know, of course, that will never

Babcock Ranch

happen. That horse would just as soon trample you into the ground as to look at you."

Anna and Avonaco exchanged smiles, and she loosened her grip on his arm. "I guess it is time to eat. Please be seated, everyone." Although she had spent the entire afternoon and early evening in preparing the meal, the ranch hands consumed it in a matter of minutes. They were complimentary about the moist tenderness of the roast and the flakiness of the biscuits. Only Jake remained silent throughout the meal. He avoided looking at her even though he sat directly across from her at the opposite end of the big table.

Most of the conversation among the ranch hands was about the number of cattle they had rounded up after they had escaped through a hole in the barbed-wire fencing.

"I think the wire was cut," said Israel, the youngest of them. "I looked at the ends of the wire, and it looked like it was a smooth cut."

Anna leaned forward, resting her elbows on the table. "Who would do such a thing?"

Babcock Ranch

The others looked toward Jake. Anna detected a slight shake of his head and a look that flashed in his eyes warning them to remain silent.

She was determined to avoid being left out of any conversation about the ranch. "Jake, what is going on?"

She watched as Jake drew in a deep breath. For the first time, he looked directly into her eyes. "It's nothing we can't handle."

Anna persisted. "Has this happened before?"

David, another of the ranch-hands, looked at her. "Almost weekly since the government did away with the use of public lands and required fencing of the lands privately owned."

Anna frowned. "I don't understand the connection."

Jake chuckled. "How could you? I am certain our problems out here never appeared in the society section of New York newspapers."

Anna shoved her chair back from the table and was about to lash out at Jake, but Avonaco covered her tiny hand with his larger, gnarled one. "Well, I think we have taken up enough of your time, little Archisa. I will stay behind and help with the clean-up." With a toss

Babcock Ranch

of his head toward the door, he indicated the others should leave.

"We ride out early, tomorrow. Best we get to bed soon." He looked over at Jake, who immediately shoved his chair back and headed for the door.

Jake stomped across the room and yanked the door open. He turned and faced Anna. "You won't have to fix breakfast or lunch. I will take care of it out on the range."

"I don't mind fixing the other meals, Jake."

"I said I would take care of it." He whirled around and stomped out onto the porch.

Anna looked at Avonaco. "He hates me."

Avonaco took her hand in his. "No, Archisa. He does not hate you. He fears you."

She stared into the dark, penetrating eyes of her lifelong mentor and friend. "He's afraid I will sell the ranch."

"No. He fears you because you have become a beautiful woman."

Babcock Ranch

Chapter 6

Anna lay looking out the window of her bedroom at the full moon. Suddenly, she heard the sound she had prayed to hear. Jumping up and putting on her robe, she rushed toward the kitchen. She grabbed a lantern, quickly lit it, and headed outside. Maximus followed her out the door. "You may come with me, Maximus, but you must not bark or chase after him."

When she reached the pasture, she saw him. The moonlight bounced off his fiery red coat and highlighted the outline of his muscular body. He had grown and was even more beautiful and majestic than she remembered. Suddenly, Maximus ran past her yipping and wagging his tail so hard he zigzagged across the pasture. "Maximus, stop. You'll frighten him away."

To her amazement, the giant horse lowered his head and let the exuberant Maximus lick his face and excitedly run back and forth between his powerful legs—legs that with one kick could have sent the dog to his death. Anna sat down on the ground and watched the

Babcock Ranch

reunion of the two apparent friends. So, he sent Maximus to me. He knew I had returned and would take care of his friend.

After several minutes of playful interactions with Maximus, the horse raised his proud head and looked directly at her.

Jake had also heard the piercing whinny and had grabbed his rifle. Outside of the bunkhouse, Avonaco stopped him. "Put the gun down, Jake. You won't need it."

Jake stared toward the pasture at the silhouette of the colossal horse. "He is something, isn't he? Even from this distance, he appears enormous." Just then he noticed Anna sitting on the ground facing the powerful animal. "What is she doing? He will surely charge and trample her." He raised the gun and aimed it at the horse. "One move toward her, and he is dead."

Avonaco grabbed the barrel of the gun and yanked it out of his hands. "Watch and learn, Jake. She is in no danger."

The stallion slowly walked toward Anna, and she held out her hand to him. She stood and gracefully began circling in the tall grass. The

Babcock Ranch

giant horse followed her every move—twisting and turning as she did and trailing her path through small and large circles.

To Jake, it appeared as if they were dancing. He marveled at the grace and beauty of both creatures. After several minutes, Anna stopped and faced the horse. She pointed to the ground, and the magnificent being knelt. She quickly slid onto his back and wove his long, flowing mane through her fingers. The horse raised and began to lope around in concentric circles that widened with each rotation. After several rounds, Anna let loose of his mane and spread her arms out to the side maintaining complete balance as the horse began to increase his speed. The two moved as one, spotlighted by the light of the full moon.

Jake had never seen anything like the apparent melding of two bodies into one. He realized he was witnessing the same images she had painted. Anna's dark hair flowed behind her, and her paleness was even more pronounced in the soft light. A lump formed in his throat. "It's like watching something spiritual." His voice was husky and full of emotion.

Babcock Ranch

Avonaco nodded. "It is spiritual. Two spirits have become one."

After several minutes, the horse slowed until he gradually stopped.

He knelt again, and Anna slid down from his back. She wrapped her arms around his giant neck and leaned against him for several moments before stepping away. Jake heard her voice, but he could not understand what she said to the horse.

For several minutes, Maximus rushed first toward Anna then abruptly ran back to the stallion. He appeared confused about whether to stay with the horse or to follow Anna back to the house. The stallion gently nudged him with his giant head, pushing him away and toward Anna.

Jake shook his head. He was baffled and overcome by what he had witnessed. "Avonaco, what is going on here? I have never seen anything like that in my life."

"And you won't see it anywhere but here. You see, Jake, that horse was born on this ranch when Anna was just a young girl. The mare died during his birth, and Anna took it on herself to bottle feed and care for the little colt. She named him Luna because of the full moon

Babcock Ranch

the night he was born. She slept in the barn with him for weeks and spent every waking hour talking to him, leading him around, and nurturing him. Every night they would dance in the moonlight just as you saw them tonight. The bond between the two of them is greater than any I have ever seen."

Jake frowned. "If that is so, why is he now living in the mountains?"

Avonaco rested his hand on Jake's shoulder. "Because Anna knew his spirit. Even his birth indicated he was destined to live on his own. She knew from the beginning he was meant to be free. So, on the night before she left for New York, under a full moon, she led him to the pasture, and after they finished their dance, she whispered something to him much like she did tonight. He reared, let out a mournful whinny, and ran for the mountains. Tonight, is the first time he has returned to the ranch since she set him free."

Jake stared out at the now empty pasture. "Incredible. When the next full moon appears, will he come again?"

Avonaco nodded. "Yes. I do not doubt as long as she is here, he will continue to come to her. That is unless Colonel Holloway's men

Babcock Ranch

have their way with him. Come. We have an early day tomorrow.

We must rest."

Jake followed him back inside, but he knew he would not sleep

tonight.

Babcock Ranch

Chapter 7

Anna placed the blank canvas on the easel. It was the first moment she had to paint since she arrived at the ranch. An image was burning in her mind, and she wanted to capture it before the inspiration vanished. She had not felt the intense desire to paint for some time; not since she had painted the four canvases of Luna. Even in New York, painting had become work, not a passion. She had painted what would sell, not what she felt. Survival had been the motivation for painting rather than imagination and pleasure. But after last night, her passion returned.

She lightly sketched the image on the canvas then mixed the paint colors she needed. As she painted, everything in her immediate world vanished. Her reality became the scene coming to life before her. Several hours passed without her realizing it. Not until Maximus ran toward the door and began loudly barking, did she look up from the canvas.

Babcock Ranch

"What is it, Maximus?" She resented the invasion of reality into the world she was creating, but she forced herself to get up and walk over to the kitchen window to see what was causing Maximus so much anxiety. In the distance, she saw a single rider racing toward the house. The muscles in her body tensed and her heart raced. "Not again." She glanced over at Maximus. He appeared more excited than wary. She glanced out the window again. The rider was closer now, and she was relieved to discover it wasn't Colonel Holloway. "It's my friend, Courtney Livingston, Maximus."

Anna walked out onto the porch to meet her. Courtney slid her horse to an abrupt stop and jumped down from his back. The horse was covered in white sweat and breathing heavily. "What's the emergency, Courtney? Your poor horse looks exhausted. Did you gallop him all the way here?"

Courtney loosened the girth and pulled off the saddle. "I did. I hated to do it, but I had to get something to you right away, and I have to get back to town before Colonel Holloway knows I'm gone." She reached into the saddlebag and handed Anna a newspaper. "Look at

Babcock Ranch

the front page while I get this poor horse out of the sun. I need to

walk him and cool him down."

As they walked toward the barn, Anna read the headlines. "What am

I looking for, Courtney?"

"Look at what I circled on the second page."

Anna skimmed the page. She suddenly stopped. "Oh no, Courtney.

Do you think my grandmother is on this list?"

Courtney faced her. "I checked, and she is. I knew I had to get this to

you right away. Your grandmother never subscribed to the Gazette

so you wouldn't have known what was going on. You only have two

weeks before the county sells the ranch for delinquent taxes. If you

don't pay the back taxes before the deadline, you'll lose everything."

Anna plopped down on a bale of hay next to the barn and read the

notice aloud.

> Notice is hereby given that the following list contains
> the names of persons and the property description
> upon which the taxes for the year 1897 are delinquent
> with the amount of taxes and costs due, opposite each
> name; Unless the taxes so delinquent as aforesaid,
> together with the costs, and percentages are paid prior
> thereto; the real property upon which said taxes are a

Babcock Ranch

> lien, will be sold at public auction on July 30, 1897
> between the hours of ten o'clock a.m. and two
> o'clock p.m. or on such other dates to which the sale
> may be postponed within the limit fixed by the law in
> front of the County Treasurers Office at the Court
> House of said County in Billings, Montana
> Given under my hand this day of June 1, A.D. 1897
> S.F. Morse
> County Treasurer of Yellowstone County, Montana

She held her breath as she frantically searched for her grandmother's name among the two-page list. Several charges of $400 for 160 acres jumped off the page. Her grandmother owned 1200 acres. Based on that rate per acre, Anna calculated the amount she would probably have to pay, but the total seemed unrealistic. Surely, her mental calculation was wrong. She couldn't imagine she would owe so much. When she finally found her grandmother's name she gasped.

"Oh, my god, Courtney. I don't have that kind of money."

Anna's mind darted in a thousand different directions. Her heart thumped hard against her chest as if it were trying to leave her body. She had no understanding of taxes or other financial matters, but one thing was clear. She was about to lose the ranch her grandparents

Babcock Ranch

and parents died for. Her decision to sell the ranch was weakening, and the possibility of losing it to land speculators was unthinkable. Courtney felt Anna's despair. "Your grandmother used to complain about her taxes all the time, but somehow she always managed to pay them. I feel certain she would have put money aside to plan for this. Have you checked the bank to see if she had an account?"

Anna jumped up and began to pace in circles wringing her hands. "No, I haven't checked with the bank. She didn't trust banks and for as long as I can remember she kept her money here, hidden away somewhere."

Courtney laid her hand on her horse's withers. "He's cooled down. Can I put him in a stall to feed and water him while I'm here?"

"Of course."

As they walked back to the house, neither of them spoke. Once inside, Anna mechanically went through the motions of pouring tea and setting sugar and some biscuits on the table.

Courtney watched her as she automatically did what was expected in welcoming a guest into one's home. When Anna finally sat down,

Babcock Ranch

Courtney patted her hand. "Maybe this isn't as bad as we think it is. Surely you know where your grandmother kept her money?"

Anna slumped back against her chair and shook her head. "I was so young, and money matters were not important to me. I was too wrapped up in Luna to pay attention to what was going on around me. I have no idea where she might have hidden money. All I know is she didn't trust banks. I don't remember anything else."

"I wish I could help you, Sweetie, but I am barely keeping my head above water as it is. Between my monthly payments to Colonel Holloway and keeping my store well-stocked, I struggled this time to pay my taxes."

Anna looked up. "Courtney, what do you know about Colonel Holloway?"

Courtney wrinkled her forehead. "Have you met the town's largest property owner and shrewdest businessman?"

Anna nodded. "Unfortunately, I have." She related her encounter with him in town and at the ranch. "I don't trust him, Courtney. I worry he might cheat you out of your business."

Babcock Ranch

Courtney got up and walked over to the fireplace. "Don't worry about me. I can handle my own against him, but you might be in trouble. He doesn't hesitate to squash anyone who crosses him." She picked up one of Anna's paintings of Luna and studied it. "These are exquisite, Anna. I know I could sell them for you."

"They are not for sale."

Courtney faced her. "Not even if they will pay your taxes?"

Anna's eyes opened wide. "Do you think you could sell them for that much? I am not Van Gogh or Monet. I am an unknown artist."

"Hopefully, you won't be unknown forever." Courtney glanced through the window at the sun as it descended toward the western mountains. "I've got to be going. Colonel Holloway will be stopping by the Mercantile for his monthly payment, and I wouldn't want him to know I snuck away to bring you the bad news. I feel certain he is counting on you not knowing about your situation. He would love to get hold of your ranch."

Anna grabbed Courtney and hugged her. "I can't thank you enough for letting me know. I guess I have some searching to do."

Babcock Ranch

Courtney smiled. "Yes, you do. Let me know about your paintings."

"I will."

Courtney headed for the door then looked back. "Anna, Colonel Holloway is a dangerous man. I think it would be best if he didn't find out we are friends, especially after your encounters with him."

Anna raised an eyebrow. "For my sake, or yours?"

Courtney looked away from Anna's penetrating eyes. "I wish I could say for both of our sakes, but you could always tell when I was lying." She raised her head and looked directly at her friend. "For my sake; at least until I pay off my loan. He is vindictive, and I have worked too hard to get where I am."

Anna forced a smile. "I understand."

Courtney fled out the door to escape the disappointment reflected in Anna's eyes.

Maximus leaned against Anna's skirt, and she gently patted his head. "Well, Maximus, I guess you, Luna and Avonaco are my only friends." She straightened her shoulders and headed for her

Babcock Ranch

Grandmother's parlor. "Come on, Maximus. We are going on a treasure hunt."

Babcock Ranch

Chapter 8

After supper, Anna asked Avonaco and Jake to stay behind for a few minutes once the others had gone. She had spent most of the afternoon searching through her grandmother's desk, the herb cellar, and every room in the house hoping to find hidden money, but she found nothing.

Avonaco leaned his elbows on the table. "You were very quiet during dinner, Archisa. Is something troubling you?"

She handed him the newspaper and pointed to her grandmother's name among the list of delinquent taxpayers. Without saying a word, he passed the article on to Jake.

Jake looked at it and tossed the paper back to her. "It is wrong."

Anna stiffened. "Why do you say that? I am certain the County Treasurer keeps accurate records. He wouldn't make this type of mistake."

Jake leaned toward her. "You are naive. Morse is a puppet. He does whatever Holloway tells him to do."

Babcock Ranch

Anna shook her head. "But the taxes were due after Granny passed away. She couldn't possibly have paid them."

Jake rolled his eyes. "Of course she couldn't have paid them at the time they were due, but she did pay them."

Avonaco nodded. "I agree with Jake. Your grandmother knew she was going to leave this earth long before she did." He took Anna's hand in his. "Archisa, your grandmother was a savvy businesswoman. She wouldn't have failed to make sure all of her affairs were in order before she died. She would not have wanted to leave you saddled with any debts."

Anna looked at Jake. "How can you be so sure she paid her taxes?"

Jake crossed his arms over his chest and pushed his chair back on two legs. "Because I took her to the County Treasurers Office a week before she died."

Anna sighed. "Just because you took her there doesn't prove anything. Must you always be so cryptic in your answers, Jake? Did you go into the Treasurer's office with her and actually see her hand him the money?"

Babcock Ranch

Jake let his chair fall forward on all four legs. He leaned his elbows on the table and stared into Anna's eyes. "No, I did not go in with her, but she showed me the receipt and told me where she intended to put it for safekeeping."

Anna waited for him to disclose where her grandmother had put the receipt, but he said nothing more. "For Pete's sake Jake, must I wrench ever detail from you?"

Jake chuckled. "Old habits die hard. Never divulge everything you know at once."

"What is that supposed to mean?"

"It's a long, boring story."

Anna jumped up from the table. "Jake, where did she put the receipt?"

"I figured you knew where she kept her important papers and money. Don't tell me you don't remember. You haven't been gone from here that long."

Anna looked away. "It's not that I don't remember. I just never knew. I admit I should have paid more attention to that sort of thing,

Babcock Ranch

but I didn't. I have spent the whole day searching this entire house and the cellar. I have no idea where she might have kept such things."

Jake pushed away from the table. "At least you admit your ignorance. Come on. I'll show you."

Anna and Avonaco followed him into her grandmother's parlor. Jake opened Granny's writing desk and pulled out one of the drawers. He reached behind it and removed a panel exposing a small door with a keyhole. "Her papers and money are behind this fake panel."

Anna leaned in close to peer into the desk. Her hand accidentally brushed against Jake's, and he quickly withdrew it.

"Where is the key to the locked door, Jake?

"Patience. I was getting to that."

Anna touched his arm and felt him flinch. He quickly whirled around and walked to the other side of the room. As he passed by her canvas, he hesitated and lifted the cloth covering the painting. He leaned in close to examine it. Anna quickly yanked the cloth back over the painting.

Babcock Ranch

"I don't like to share my unfinished work."

Jake smiled. "And you criticize me for being reticent?"

"The key, Jake? Where is it?"

He picked up a portrait of Luna that Anna had painted years ago.

"Fitting she would choose to hide your key here, don't you think?"

He flipped the painting over, and pulling a knife from his pocket, he loosened the metal screws holding the frame in place. A small key dropped into his hand.

He tossed the key to her. "Here you go."

Avonaco laid his hand on Jake's shoulder. "Perhaps we should leave Archisa alone to explore what her grandmother left for her."

Jake nodded. "If you find any cash, you might want to consider paying me back for your boots and riding clothes."

Anna shot him a hateful glance.

He smiled. "You're welcome by the way. Oh, and I think the background in your painting needs a little more black to add contrast."

Babcock Ranch

Anna opened her mouth but could think of nothing to say other than an insincere, "Thank you."

After they left, she rushed to the desk and inserted the key into the tiny lock. Drawing in a deep breath, she hesitated for several moments before opening the door. She rolled her eyes upward. "I hope Jake is right, Granny. Otherwise, I am in a lot of trouble down here." Carefully turning the key, she reached inside the tight space and pulled out several documents tightly rolled and tied with string. A gold wedding ring, bundles of cash, and an envelope were among the other things she found. She flipped over the envelope. It was addressed to her.

She carried the letter over to her grandmother's rocker and ran her fingertips slowly across the envelope. A tear fell onto her name, and the ink bled into the paper. With the back of her hand, she quickly wiped away the tears building up in her eyes. She held the envelope close to her nose and inhaled deeply. She detected the scent of her grandmother's favorite hand cream. Carefully she tore open the envelope. She immediately recognized Granny's elegant

Babcock Ranch

handwriting—how many nights she had spent at the kitchen table carefully copying lines of Bible verses her grandmother had chosen for the day's lesson. Granny was a stickler for perfection, insisting each letter was perfectly formed. 'You are writing God's words so they must be flawlessly and beautifully copied,' she would say. Anna began to read the letter aloud.

> My Dearest Anna,
> It is with a heavy heart that I leave you, but I know
>
> you will be all right. You are a strong, young woman
>
> and will do what is best for yourself and the ranch. I
>
> want you to make your own choice about where you
>
> will spend the rest of your life. Of course, I hope it
>
> will be here in Montana, but it must be your choice,
>
> not mine.
>
> Avonaco and Jake will be friends upon which you can
>
> rely without reservation. They are both good and
>
> honest men. Unfortunately, Billings has changed
>
> considerably since you left. You have probably

Babcock Ranch

discovered that for yourself by now. Not only the

things visible to the eye have changed, but the heart

of the city and those running it are also different from

the friends and neighbors you once knew. Greed and

corruption came with growth and progress.

You will no doubt encounter Colonel Robert

Holloway. He is a wealthy land speculator and as

black-hearted as he is tall and handsome. I know you

are perceptive and will see through his polite exterior.

Be wary of him. He is Satan in silk neckties.

Anna smiled and looked down at Maximus lying next to her feet.

"My grandmother could paint with words better than I can with oils,

Maximus. I wish you could have known her; she would have loved

you.

She returned to the letter.

You know I have always mistrusted banks. I still do.

So, I told Jake where I stored my cash and important

papers. I assume if you are reading this letter, he has

Babcock Ranch

shared that information with you. Jake is modest and will not tell you of his talents and background. He has been a godsend to his uncle and me. I am certain he won't tell you what I am about to disclose, and you probably should not let him know I told you. He gave up his law practice and left his father's firm in Chicago to come out West to help his uncle and me. I don't know what we would have done without his strength in mind and body.

Anna frowned. "Jake modest? I think not. But a lawyer? That is astonishing. I guess that explains his ambiguous responses to questions. But why the secrecy? He should be proud of his accomplishments." She shrugged and continued reading.

Among the papers you will find in my desk are the Bills of Sale for our cattle, the deed to the ranch, and the receipts for the taxes I have begrudgingly paid each year. Please keep these papers safe. I don't trust the county treasurer or Colonel Holloway. Holloway

Babcock Ranch

has had his eye on this property for years because of the water rights we have. Others are also jealous of the natural resources on the ranch.

One last thing—I have seen Luna when I have been out onto the range. Although he keeps his distance, I know he recognizes me. He is indeed an extraordinary creature, not only because of his size and beauty but because of his instincts and intelligence. I feel confident he will know when you have returned and will come to you. Be careful not to let others know he visits you. They will lay in wait for him because he has a somewhat vilified reputation as a horse thief. Perhaps, you can convince him to return to the ranch and live out his life under your care and protection.

This letter is long, but it is hard for me to end it. Finishing it is a final farewell, and it breaks my heart to know I will never again hold you in my arms. Rest

Babcock Ranch

assured I will forever watch over you even if I can't

be with you. Every summer breeze that brushes your

cheek is my kiss and every winter snowflake that

lands on you is a blessing from me.

With all my love, Sweet Anna.

Granny

Anna clutched the letter to her chest and let the tears she had held

back stream down her face. Maximus sat up and rested his front paw

on her lap. She gently patted his head. "It's okay, buddy. I need to

let these tears fall. I have held them back too long."

Babcock Ranch

Chapter 9

Jake awoke before dawn. He hadn't slept well last night or any night since Anna had arrived. Her presence on the ranch affected everything he did and felt. She disrupted his routine and scattered his thinking. Although he tried to keep her out of his mind, he couldn't. Out on the range, he worried about what she was doing on the ranch. The arrival of Maximus relieved some but not all of his fears for her safety. He could scarcely wait for supper every night and resented it when one of the other ranch hands mentioned how beautiful she was. He had almost brawled with David over an inappropriate remark he made about her. If Avonaco hadn't stepped between them, he would have unfairly taken his frustrations out on David.

Last night when she brushed against his hand and touched his arm, electric shocks ran through his entire body. Even thinking about her touch sent a rush of warmth through him. Every thought of her caused a physical reaction in him.

Babcock Ranch

When he had first met her at the train station, he had wanted her to get on the train and go back to New York, but now he was afraid she might actually leave. He couldn't let that happen, but he didn't know how to prevent it. He couldn't ask her to stay. It had to be her decision.

He finished checking the collar and harness on each of the horses hitched to the wagon and hopped onto the seat to take it up to the house. Anna hadn't mentioned going to the Treasurer's office in town this morning, but he knew she would. He couldn't let her go alone. Although she was a smart, independent woman, confrontation with Morse was bound to be nasty.

Just as he suspected, Anna stepped out onto the porch dressed in her blue traveling suit. Maximus rushed past her and leaped into the back of the wagon.

Jake's heart flipped flopped at the sight of her. He drew in a deep breath. "Are you going to clean stalls dressed like that?"

Babcock Ranch

Anna frowned and waved a piece of paper in the air. "No, of course not. I was going to leave you this note asking you to do the morning chores for me."

"I already took care of them."

"How did you know I would be going into town so early?"

"Just a hunch."

He held his hand down to help her into the wagon. She struggled to step up with her narrow skirt. He shook his head and jumped down to the ground. Swooping her up in his arms, he plopped her down on the wooden seat. "Just how did you intend to get to town in that outfit? Certainly not by horseback, and even if you could figure out how to get into the wagon in that narrow skirt, have you ever hitched a team of horses to a wagon?"

"Of course, I have; just not lately."

He shook his head. "Move over. I prefer to drive."

"You don't need to go with me. I can handle this by myself."

Babcock Ranch

"I am sure you think you can, but you need a witness, and I'm it. Now are you going to scoot over or am I going to have to move you?"

Anna stared at him for a moment then reluctantly moved to the other side of the wooden seat. As he settled himself next to her, she glanced into the back of the wagon. "Don't you have a stepping stool to help me get in and out of the wagon? When we are in town, I don't relish the thought of you picking me up and tossing me onto the seat like a sack of flour."

Jake took hold of the reins and lightly slapped them against the horses. The wagon lunged forward, and Anna fell against him. It took all his will to resist putting his arm around her to hold her next to him. "No. We never needed a stepping stool. Your grandmother could hop in and out of this wagon as quickly as I could. Of course, she dressed appropriately."

"Why must you always mock me, Jake?"

Jake shrugged. "I guess because you are mockable."

"Mockable? That isn't even a word."

Babcock Ranch

"Perhaps it should be. Would you prefer I had said 'because you are vulnerable?'"

Anna stiffened. "Vulnerable indicates I am weak, and I am not."

He glanced over at her. Why did he always feel compelled to provoke her? Around her, he behaved like a young schoolboy dipping a girl's pigtails into the inkwell to get her attention. He sighed. At this time, it was just safer to argue with her than to reveal his true feelings.

"I know you are not weak, Anna. Let's talk about something else—like how we intend to approach Morse about the taxes."

Anna pulled out a folded paper from her drawstring purse. "I think we should just show him the receipt."

"I don't think it was wise to bring it with you. What if you lose it or Morse takes it?"

Anna chuckled. "It's not the original, Jake. I'm not naïve. I found the same type of paper in Granny's desk as the original and copied the handwriting. I sketched the stamp with an ink pen." She held the document in front of his face so he could get a close look at it.

Babcock Ranch

"Impressive. It looks authentic. Maybe you should go into forgery instead of painting."

When they arrived at the Treasurer's Office, Colonel Holloway was coming out the door. He tipped his hat to her. "Good morning, Miss Babcock. What an unexpected pleasure." Anna nodded and faked a smile. From behind her, she heard Maximus growl. She placed her hand on his back. "Stay, Maximus." She could feel his raised hackles. He obeyed her and sat back on his haunches, but he never took his eyes off the Colonel.

Colonel Holloway smiled. "I see you taught your dog to obey your commands."

Jake leaned in close to her. "Do you know him?"

Anna turned away from the Colonel and faced Jake. She lowered her voice so Colonel Holloway couldn't hear her. "Yes, he visited me at the ranch the first day I arrived."

"What? You should have told me."

Babcock Ranch

"I handled it. Now come around here and help me down before Colonel Holloway tries to help me. I can't guarantee I can keep Maximus from jumping on him again."

Jake stared at her with bulging eyes and his mouth gaping. She nudged him with her elbow, and he immediately hopped out of the wagon. He reached up to lift her down, but she took hold of his hand and managed to jump to the ground gracefully.

She faced Colonel Holloway. "Colonel, I assume you know my foreman, Jake Crowley?"

Colonel Holloway nodded. "I do, indeed. Nice to see you again Jake." He offered Jake his hand.

Jake hesitated but finally shook it. "Good morning, Colonel. I am sorry we can't linger, but we have business with Mr. Morse." He watched the Colonel closely to see his reaction upon hearing of their meeting with Morse, but Holloway showed no sign of concern or surprise.

The Colonel smiled. "Well, then, I mustn't keep you any longer." He looked at Anna. "I am still hoping to have the carriage ride you

Babcock Ranch

promised. I must apologize for how things ended last time. I assure you it won't happen again."

Anna curtsied without responding. She possessively linked her arm with Jake's and leaned in close to him.

Jake felt her tremble. He immediately put his hand over hers and gently squeezed it. As they climbed the stairs to the Treasurer's office, he glanced back at the Colonel and was not surprised to see the anger in his eyes. Jake tightened his hold on Anna's hand.

"Anna, what was Holloway apologizing for?

"I'll explain later. Right now, let's concentrate on getting Morse to correct the error on Granny's taxes."

Jake sneered. "Error? Is that going to be your approach? What he did was no error; it was an intentional act of fraud."

Anna squeezed his arm. "You capture more flies with honey than with vinegar, Jake."

When they entered the Treasurer's Office, a male clerk greeted them.

"Good morning, can I help you?"

Anna smiled. "We are here to see Mr. Morse."

Babcock Ranch

"Do you have an appointment?"

Anna lightly touched the clerk's hand. "No. I didn't realize I would need an appointment with him. He is a public servant, is he not?"

The clerk stared down at her gloved hand resting on his. His face reddened. "Why yes he is, but he is a very busy man and sometimes unable to accommodate unexpected visitors."

Anna pushed her lips into a pout. She patted the clerk's hand. "If you don't mind, I'll just peek into his office. I am certain he will be glad to see me."

Without waiting for the clerk to respond, she moved quickly over to the office door and entered Morse's office.

Jake smiled at the flustered clerk. "Thanks for your help."

Mr. Morse looked up from a stack of papers and yanked the big cigar from his mouth. He rested the cigar on the edge of a large, wooden humidor. "May I help you? Has my clerk left the office?"

Anna noticed the excessive elegance of the big office. It was not at all what she expected of a public-supported, government office. Velvet drapes hung from the windows, and thick woolen rugs

Babcock Ranch

covered the floor. Beautiful ornate carvings decorated the front panel of Mr. Morse's massive mahogany desk. Leather bound books filled the floor to ceiling walnut bookshelves. Four horseshoe-shaped, leather and wood desk chairs resting on carved tulip legs encircled a large mahogany table near the bookshelves. It looked more like the office of a wealthy, business tycoon than of a government employee. She gracefully sat on the edge of one of the button-backed leather wing-chairs facing Mr. Morse and motioned for Jake to sit next to her.

 "My esteemed, Mr. Morse, I am sorry to barge in like this, sir, but you have made a grave error by including my property on your list of delinquent taxpayers in the Gazette yesterday."

Mr. Morse frowned. "I don't make mistakes like that. I recognize Mr. Crowley, but who are you?"

Anna raised her hand to cover her mouth. "Oh, how rude of me. Please forgive me, but I have been so distraught after seeing my deceased, beloved grandmother's name on the list I have forgotten

Babcock Ranch

all propriety." She pulled a lace handkerchief from her sleeve and dabbed at her eyes. "I am Anna Babcock."

Mr. Morse's face immediately reddened. He squirmed in his chair and cleared his throat several times. Anna watched him closely as he appeared to struggle to regain control from the apparent shock of her presence. After several seconds, he rested his elbows on his desk and leaned toward her. "Let me first offer my condolences on your grandmother's passing. Billings will miss her."

Anna dabbed her eyes again.

"I am sorry to have upset you, Miss Babcock. It is dreadfully unfortunate your grandmother passed away before the taxes were due and thus failed to pay them. Unless you are here to pay the amount owed, I fear I can do nothing but to follow the law I swore to uphold."

Anna pulled the receipt from her purse. "I am sure you are an honest, law-abiding citizen, Mr. Morse. Otherwise, you could not have been elected to such an important position, isn't that right?"

Babcock Ranch

Mr. Morse puffed out his chest. "Not intending to boast, but yes, that is true. I am quite proud of my integrity."

Jake was enjoying the drama playing out in front of him. Anna set Morse up perfectly.

She carefully unfolded the receipt and slid it across the desk to Mr. Morse. "Well then, I am sure it must have been a clerk's error in not posting the early payment my grandmother made on her taxes."

Mr. Morse hesitated then picked up the receipt.

Anna looked at Jake. "Wasn't it just a week before Granny died that you carried her here in the wagon to pay her taxes?"

Jake nodded. "You are right. She showed me that receipt when she came out of the office."

Beads of sweat formed on Mr. Morse's forehead. He ran his finger around the inside of his shirt collar and flexed the muscles in his shoulders. He stood up and walked over to one of the bookshelves holding large, leather-bound audit books. He pulled one from the shelf and carried it back to his desk. "I am sorry, but I have no recall of your grandmother's visit. If she made a payment, I will find it in

Babcock Ranch

this ledger." He flipped through the pages and once more checked the date on the receipt. "Ah, here is the list of payments made on the same date as written on your receipt. He ran his finger down the list of entries."

Anna noticed his finger trembled.

"I am sorry, I don't see any entry for your grandmother. He started to close the book, but Anna quickly put her hand on the page. "Since this is a public record, I prefer to check the list myself, Mr. Morse." She dragged her finger down the column of entries. He was right. She found no listing for her grandmother.

Mr. Morse quickly closed the book and carried it back to the shelf. As he returned to his desk, Anna blocked his way. She placed her hand on the lapel of his jacket. "Mr. Morse, you and I both know my grandmother paid you the amount written on that receipt, and if you don't immediately rectify this situation, you will find yourself facing a judge and jury, and your so-called integrity will lead you straight to jail."

Babcock Ranch

Mr. Morse pulled himself up to his full height and glared at her. "I would appreciate it if you both would leave my office. I have done nothing wrong, and unless you have the money to pay the back taxes, your ranch will be auctioned off in two weeks."

Anna smiled and reached for the receipt. Mr. Morse jerked it out of her hands and tore it into pieces. He tossed it into the wastebasket and using the hot end of his smoldering cigar, he set it on fire.

Jake grabbed him by the front of his starched white shirt. "You little weasel. I suspect that Holloway is involved in this somehow too. If he is, I will make sure you both rot in state prison."

Morse smirked and motioned to the burning paper. "You no longer have any evidence to support your accusation." He tossed his head toward Anna. "It will be her word against mine, and who do you think the judge will favor—a woman or me?"

Jake shoved him hard against the wall.

Anna pulled Jake away from Mr. Morse. "Jake let's go. The Court House closes at noon. It is apparent the next time we meet Mr. Morse it will be in a courtroom." She ran her hand over Mr. Morse's

Babcock Ranch

shirt to smooth it and smiled up at him. "I know, Mr. Morse, you think you burned my evidence, but you are wrong." She linked her arm with Jakes, and they left the office.

Once outside, Jake whirled her around to face him. "Are you sure you didn't study acting in New York? You were amazing. I only wish you hadn't indicated you had more evidence. I know Holloway is somehow involved in all this. He's evil by nature, and Morse is a cornered skunk. Both of them are dangerous."

Anna held her hands out in front of her. They trembled. "I was so angry I didn't think about that."

Jake took her hands in his. "You certainly appeared calm and completely in control."

"I wasn't. Can you believe the dishonesty of that man? Now, what do we do?"

"Just as you said. We go to the Court House to request an injunction to stop the sale of your property and file a civil lawsuit against Morse and possibly Holloway. You can leave Act Two of this mess to me."

Babcock Ranch

"Are you licensed to practice in Montana?" The minute the words came out of her mouth she realized she revealed the information in Granny's letter.

Jake looked at her closely and raised an eyebrow. "So, something you got from Granny last night let the cat out of the bag, did it?"

"I'm sorry, Jake. In a letter to me, Granny explained you gave up your law practice to come to Montana to help your uncle. She also warned me not to mention it to you, but I'm so nervous right now it just slipped out. Why don't you want anyone to know you are a lawyer?"

Jake shrugged. "I prefer to keep that part of my life in the past. I would rather be known as a ranch hand out here. Life is less complicated that way."

"Does anyone else know?"

"Avonaco, and now you. Of course, as soon as I file a lawsuit at the Court House, all of Billings will know. Lucky for you, I can practice in Montana."

Babcock Ranch

She lightly touched his arm. "Jake, I'm sorry to drag you into this mess, but I am truly grateful you are here to help me through it." Jake stared into her eyes, and his heart jumped into his throat. He wanted to pull her in his arms and vow to protect her forever, but he didn't.

Babcock Ranch

Chapter 10

Sam Morse yelled for his clerk. "Henry, why did you let Crowley and Miss Babcock into my office without checking first with me?"

"I didn't let them in, sir. The woman just swooped past me and opened your door. She said you would be glad to see her, so I didn't try to stop her." He glanced over at the smoldering papers in the waste can. "Shall I take the can outside, sir?"

Morse glared at the smoke rising from the brass waste can. "You can't just pick it up and carry it out of here. It's hot. Get something to wrap around it and take it outside to dump it."

Henry immediately slipped off his suit coat. He wrapped it around the waste can and headed out the door.

Morse paced behind his desk. He had no idea anyone would know about Mrs. Babcock's payment. She always came into town alone. He recalled her visit quite vividly. He had tried to avoid giving her a receipt by explaining Henry had left for the day, and he would send her a receipt later, but she had insisted he give her one right then.

Babcock Ranch

She had stood over him and watched him write it out. He wrinkled his forehead. "The Colonel is going to be furious when I tell him about the receipt."

He stopped and shrugged. But the receipt no longer exists; I burned it. Miss Babcock was simply bluffing when she indicated she had other evidence.

Henry returned with the charred waste can. "I tried to clean this, Mr. Morse, but I fear it is ruined."

Mr. Morse stared at him and a smile spread across his face as a solution to his dilemma flashed into his mind. "I'll take care of it, Henry. I have something else for you to do." He pulled the ledger book he had shown Anna Babcock from the shelf and turned to the page that matched the date on the receipt she had shown him. "You evidently failed to include the payment for the Babcock property on this page. Miss Babcock showed me her grandmother's receipt with this date on it."

Henry frowned. "When I saw Mrs. Babcock's name on the list of delinquent taxpayers, I wondered why she hadn't paid her taxes;

Babcock Ranch

then I remembered she died before they were due. Begging your pardon, sir, but I don't think she paid them. I didn't deposit any payment from her."

Mr. Morse massaged his forehead and drew in a deep breath. He rolled his head from side-to-side, and his neck cracked. "For God's sake Henry, do you claim to remember every deposit you make?"

"Pretty much so, sir."

"Well, you must have forgotten about this one. I remember meeting with her the evening she paid her taxes. She paid them before she died. You had already left for the day, so I filled out the receipt. I put her money in the safe with the other payments."

"But, Mr. Morse..."

Mr. Morse held up his hand to stop him. "No more buts, Henry. Just do what I told you to do." He grabbed his hat from the coat tree.

Henry stared at him. "Are you leaving, Mr. Morse?"

"Of course, I am leaving. Why else would I have put on my hat?"

"When will you be back, sir? You have quite a few appointments this afternoon."

Babcock Ranch

"I have no idea when I will be back. Offer my apologies and reschedule anyone who comes in before I return." He stormed out of his office.

When he reached Colonel Holloway's office, he nodded at Miss Collier but didn't stop to allow her to announce his arrival to the Colonel.

He burst into Holloway's office, and the Colonel whirled around in his chair to stare at him. "Sam? What is it? You're swelled up like a bullfrog and huffing and puffing like a Northern Pacific engine. I presume your condition is related to your meeting with Anna Babcock and Crowley."

Morse dropped down into the nearest chair and wiped his forehead with a handkerchief he pulled from his pocket. "What a contrast Anna Babcock presents—sweet as candy on the outside and as venomous as a rattler within."

Holloway frowned. "What happened?"

Morse swallowed hard and pulled his chair closer to the Colonel's desk. "Bottom line, she left my office with Crowley, and they were

Babcock Ranch

headed for the Court House to more than likely file a request for an injunction to block the sale of her ranch and a civil suit against me and possibly you, too."

"Me? What the hell happened?"

Morse related the details of the conversation with Anna, including her threat of having other evidence besides the receipt he had burned. "After she left, I decided I probably should enter a payment by her grandmother in case she did have some sort of evidence to prove Mrs. Babcock did pay her taxes, though I can't imagine what it would be. I had my clerk recopy the audit page and add the payment from her grandmother."

Holloway jumped up from his chair and came around to where Morse continued to mop the sweat from his face. He grabbed Morse up from the chair by the front of his shirt and leaned in so close to him that his nose almost touched that of Morse. "You bumbling fool, you have just compounded the whole mess by involving your clerk and changing the entries. Don't you realize your accounts won't balance now?"

Babcock Ranch

Morse swallowed and opened his eyes wide. "I never thought this through, I guess. What do you propose I do now?"

Holloway let loose of his shirt and shoved him down into his chair. He moved back behind his desk and paced back in forth for several minutes. Suddenly, he stopped and turned toward Morse. A smile spread across his face.

Morse frowned and wiped away more sweat. "Why are you smiling? We have a serious problem here?"

Holloway chuckled menacingly. "Not we, Morse; you have a problem. He sat down at his deck and opened a large humidor. He took a cigar then turned the walnut case around so Morse could take one. "Want a cigar? It might be the last one you ever smoke. I doubt they let you smoke in state prison."

Morse sat in stunned silence.

Holloway lit his cigar and blew the smoke toward Morse. "I can see you are confused, Sam. Let me clarify things for you. If you recall, I paid you the correct amount for the taxes on my land by check, and Henry wrote me a receipt for that payment, right?"

Babcock Ranch

Morse squirmed in his chair. "Yes, you did, but I gave you cash back from the money Mrs. Babcock paid me, so technically you didn't actually pay your taxes with your money."

"True, but I have a receipt and a check that indicates I did. Because my ranch is smaller than hers, my taxes were less, so there must have been money left over from her payment after you gave me back my tax money. I assume you spent the leftover cash on your lavish office, or you still have the extra cash somewhere, right?" He leaned back and took a long draw on the cigar. "There's nothing more relaxing than a good cigar." He nudged the humidor closer to Morse. "Are you sure you don't want one?"

Morse swatted the humidor and sent it crashing to the floor. He jumped up from his chair and leaned over the desk at Holloway. "You are as much a part of this as I am. Hell, it was your idea in the first place to hold off entering her payment and wait to see if she died before the tax deadline so it would appear reasonable that she hadn't paid them. It was nice of her to accommodate you by dying before the taxes were due."

Babcock Ranch

Holloway flashed a smug smile. "I am a gambler my friend, and she handed me the jackpot."

Morse loosened his tie. "Yes, I remember. You were jubilant when she died before the payment deadline. Without a record of her payment, you knew Henry would automatically add her to the delinquent taxpayers list, which then allows you to buy her property at the auction for pennies on the dollar." He pounded his fist on the desk. "If you expect me to take the fall on this alone, you are seriously mistaken. I won't hesitate to drag you down with me."

Holloway reached in his desk drawer and pulled out a small pistol. He spun it around on his trigger finger and stared up at Morse. "All of that is true, Sam, but you can't prove any of it. I have a legitimate paper trail; you don't. Now that you have told your clerk to add Mrs. Babcock's name to the registry, unless you can come up with enough money to cover her payment, you are going to jail. And if you don't add her name to the registry and her granddaughter can prove her grandmother paid her taxes and there is no deposit of the money, you

Babcock Ranch

are going to jail. To add to your worries, if the Babcock ranch is not auctioned off in two weeks, I'm going to shoot you."

He pointed the pistol at Morse. "You should have stuck to the plan to leave Mrs. Babcock's name off the ledger and pray her beautiful granddaughter is bluffing about having other evidence of her grandmother's payment. Too bad you dragged your clerk into this. If he follows your order to add Mrs. Babcock's name on the accounting ledger, he's going to snoop around looking for the money. What you do about him is up to you. He knows too much. I'd shoot him if it were up to me."

He pulled back the hammer on the pistol. "Now pick up my cigars and get out of my office. I don't want to see your face around here again."

Morse walked over to the pile of cigars, and with his boot, he ground the cigars into the rug. He stormed out of the office, slamming the door behind him. When he entered the reception area, Miss Collier scurried to her desk clutching a notepad to her chest.

Babcock Ranch

Chapter 11

Avonaco and the other ranch hands were moving some of the cattle from high ground down to the lower pastures. Avonaco was riding drag—keeping the slower animals in the rear moving forward. He flinched and instinctively ducked as a series of sharp cracks from a rifle echoed through the mountains. When the gunshots ceased, the mournful whinny of a horse filled the silence. He recognized the whinny and yelled for David, who was riding on the east flank. David quickly whirled his horse around to drop back to the rear of the herd. "Sounds like Holloway's men are after that stallion again. From the sound of his whinny, they must have hit him."

Avonaco nodded. "The shots sounded like they were close, so the shooters must be on our property. I'm going to find out."

David looked at him with concern. "Let me come with you. They are a mean bunch and won't hesitate to shoot you, especially you being Cheyenne."

Babcock Ranch

Avonaco shook his head and spurred his horse into a full gallop. As he sped across the prairie, another round of shots rang out, but this time he didn't hear a whinny. His thoughts were about Anna. Her love for Luna was absolute. Without a doubt, it was Luna who brought her home. She didn't have to come back to Montana to sell the ranch. She could have arranged that from New York. If something happens to that horse, nothing will keep her here, even though she belongs here. She is light in the darkness that enshrouds the ranch since her grandmother and Jake's uncle passed. Avonaco knew Jake was falling in love with her though he won't admit it. If she leaves, he will follow her, and the Babcock Ranch will disappear.

He leaned forward in the saddle and encouraged his horse to gallop faster. Perhaps Luna had only been injured. If so, Avonaco was certain the horse would try to get back to the ranch. He squinted hard to detect any movement above him, but he saw nothing. He pulled up on the reins, and his horse slid to a stop. Swinging down from the saddle, he knelt and pressed his ear firmly against the ground. He

Babcock Ranch

closed his eyes and concentrated on listening for the sound of galloping horses pounding against the hard ground. The sounds grew louder as he listened, warning him the riders were coming his direction. He scrambled up from the ground and looked around for a place to hide until they passed. Grabbing the reins, he clambered up a steep incline pulling his reluctant horse behind him.

When he finally reached some level ground, he ducked behind a large boulder with his horse. He could see three riders now—too many for him to safely confront even though they were on Babcock property. David was right. They would not hesitate to shoot him because he was Cheyenne. Although most of the whites in Billings accepted him as an equal, others who had lost relatives during the Indian Wars blamed him for their deaths and often spat at him when he went alone into town. He knew Holloway's men were among those who despised him for who he was. He pulled his rifle from the sheath attached to his saddle. He hoped he would not have to use the gun, but he wanted to be ready in case he did.

Babcock Ranch

His muscles were taut and his palms damp. He held his breath when one of the riders slowed as they passed near where he hid above him. The man leaned over his saddle and stared at the ground. He hopped down and knelt next to the hoof prints left by Avonaco's horse. Avonaco recognized the man. Tom Jacobs was Holloway's foreman. Avonaco aimed his gun at Jacobs and placed his finger on the trigger. Jacobs knew horses, and he would know the prints on the ground were from a shod horse. The stallion would not make indentations of horseshoes.

Jacobs stood and looked up at the steep path, before climbing back into the saddle. Avonaco held his breath. He could easily have shot Jacobs, but he didn't, even though he knew if the situation were reversed, Jacobs would not have hesitated to shoot him.

Jacobs urged his horse toward the steep slope, but the horse balked and reared. He avoided falling to the ground and slapped his horse hard across the withers with his reins. The horse reared again. After several more failed attempts to get his horse to climb the incline, Jacobs finally cursed and raced away to catch up with the others.

Babcock Ranch

Avonaco lowered his gun and wiped his sweaty brow with the sleeve of his shirt.

When they rode past him, Avonaco noticed Holloway's men held their rifles in their hands. That was a good sign. They must not have found Luna or his body, and they were still looking for him. He was relieved they were headed north. The ranch was south, and if Luna wasn't dead or so badly wounded that he couldn't traverse the treacherous southern passage, he would circle back and head south to reach the ranch.

Avonaco quickly climbed into the saddle and headed his horse to higher grounds. The climb to the southern passage was steep and treacherous. Halfway up, he jumped down from the saddle and led his horse up a narrow incline. He was grateful for the surefootedness of his mount. Each morning, the ranch hands chose their horse from the herd on the ranch. He had chosen wisely today. Other horses were younger and more skittish, and he would not have been able to make the climb with them.

Babcock Ranch

Finally reaching the summit, he mounted his horse and headed south.

A few feet from where he had started, he saw drops of fresh red

blood on the ground.

Babcock Ranch

Chapter 12

It was late afternoon before Anna and Jake arrived back at the ranch.

Jake had effortlessly completed the process of filing the necessary

papers for the injunction and the lawsuit against Morse. As of yet, he

decided they had no grounds for filing a suit against Holloway.

Later, as the ranch hands entered the house for supper, Anna stepped

onto the porch and looked toward the bunkhouse for Avonaco and

Jake. She didn't see them. "David, where are Avonaco and Jake?"

David cleared his throat. "Don't you worry none, Miss Anna. I'm

sure everything is all right. They'll be along soon. I'm certain of it."

Anna wrinkled her brow. "Soon? Where are they and why should I

not be worried?"

David looked at the other two ranch hands. They avoided meeting

his eyes and stared at the floor.

Anna touched David's arm. "David, tell me where they are."

David hesitated for several moments before responding.

Anna squeezed his arm. "David, where are they?"

Babcock Ranch

He cleared his throat and looked at her with worry shining in his eyes. "Miss Babcock, when we were bringing the cattle down from the high grounds, we heard some gunshots. We figured the Holloway men were shooting at that stallion. Avonaco thought they were on your land, so he rode off to hunt them down. He never came back."

Anna sat down in one of the dining room chairs. "I assume when we returned from town, Jake set off to hunt for him."

David nodded. "That's right. He rode out to help us with the cattle, and when we told him about the shots, the mournful whinny of the horse, and Avonaco's chasing after the Holloways, Jake wheeled his horse around and took off for the southern passage."

Anna tried to process everything at once. "You heard a mournful whinny? After the shots?"

"Yes, Mam. It was loud and pitiful. I'm guessin' they must have wounded the horse."

Anna jumped up and grabbed a lantern and her woolen shawl.

"Come on, Maximus." She fled out the door.

Babcock Ranch

David ran after her. "Miss Babcock, wait. That southern passage is dangerous even in daylight. Jake will most certainly shoot me if I let you go up there."

Anna ignored him. She ran into the barn and grabbed a saddle from the tack room. David took the saddle from her. "I'll saddle the horses. You get the first aid kit and anything else you think might be needed."

"David, you don't have to go with me. I used to ride that passage day and night for years. I know it like the back of my hand."

"Maybe so, Miss Babcock, but I don't feel like being shot by Jake. He's so in love with you he don't think straight half the time. He'd shoot me on the spot if I let you go out there alone and somethin' happened to you."

Anna stared at him with widened eyes. "What did you say?"

David smiled. "You don't know how he feels about you, do you?"

Anna shook her head.

Babcock Ranch

David smiled. "He won't admit it, but the rest of us weren't born in the woods like he thinks. He's different since you arrived on the ranch."

She shook her head. "I'm sure you're wrong, David. Jake hates me. Let's go." She looked down at Maximus. "Find Luna, Maximus."

She didn't have to say another word. Maximus shot out of the barn and headed straight across the pasture toward the southern mountain. Anna and David had to race their horses hard to keep up with him.

Babcock Ranch

Chapter 13

Jake rode for hours without finding Avonaco or Luna. During daylight, he followed a trail of blood which he assumed was from Luna, but when the sun went down, it was difficult for him to see the blood drops on the ground. Jagged rocks and narrow passages high in the mountain made it dangerous to ride in daylight and even more so at night. The light of the full moon helped somewhat but not enough. Several times his horse slipped and almost sent them careening down the side of the mountain. He dismounted and walked in front of his horse futilely trying to see dark spots on the rocks and ground that signaled he was on the right path. Dozens of side trails leading up and down the mountain led to different passages. The blood drops were the only directional guidance he had.

He was exhausted and knew his horse was too. He sat down on the ground and leaned his head against a rock. His day had started earlier than usual, and the disgusting business in town had been mentally draining. He regretted he was heading down a road he had

Babcock Ranch

sworn he would never take again. The thought of spending days in a stuffy courtroom was suffocating. For weeks now, he would be unable to be out on the open range enjoying the fresh air and the thrill of chasing down a rogue bull—doing hard work and accomplishing something tangible. No more joking with the other ranch hands and playing cards with them late into the night. Instead, he would spend his days and nights in town wading through dull accounting ledgers and other documents, questioning witnesses and arguing with another lawyer—more than likely someone of questionable integrity who had managed to unjustifiably win dozens of cases. Days would bleed into nights, and he would miss evening meals with Anna and the others.

The disquieting howls of wolves and coyotes made him uneasy. They too could be following the trail of fresh blood. Avonaco had a gun, but if it was Luna's blood on the trail, the horse would be too weak by now to fight off an attack from a pack of wolves, just as he had been years ago in Chicago. Though he tried to suppress the nightmare that had been his last day in court, the memory crept into

Babcock Ranch

his mind like a slinking wolf about to pounce on his victim. An innocent man was hung because he failed to fend off a team of deceitful lawyers, lying witnesses, and a dishonest judge. What if the case against Morse turns out the same? What would Anna think of him if he was the cause of her losing her ranch?

By now she would know that he and Avonaco were missing. He prayed she wouldn't try to find them, but if she thought Luna had been injured, he knew nothing would stop her from searching for him. He hoped David could prevent her from leaving the ranch, but he doubted she would listen to him. Thinking of her in the mountains on a strange horse at night made him shudder.

He jumped up from the ground and swung himself into the saddle urging his wary horse forward. They slowly plodded ahead, stopping now and then for him to get down and touch a dark spot on the ground to verify it was blood, and that they were following the right path.

After several miles across the rough terrain, a slight whiff of smoke aroused his senses. He prayed that it was coming from a fire built by

Babcock Ranch

Avonaco rather than one made by Holloway's men. He had seen them on a trail below him not too long ago. They had apparently not given up on their search for Luna.

He tied his horse to a sturdy limb jutting out from a rock and continued on foot using the methods Avonaco taught him to keep his approach undetected. Carefully placing each foot firmly atop loose stones to keep them from sliding and avoiding fallen twigs or other debris on the path, he crept toward the scent of the smoke. As he drew closer, he could see the fire, but he didn't see anyone nearby— what he did see sickened him. Luna's massive body lay motionless on the ground. He slowly moved toward the horse but instantly froze when he felt the cold barrel of a gun shoved against his back.

"You did well, Jake, but you should have been quieter before you got so close. I heard you coming long before you got off your horse. Sounds echo in the mountain."

Jake whirled around to face Avonaco. "You do realize you just shortened my life by at least ten years."

Babcock Ranch

"Come, I have been trying to save Luna, but he has lost a lot of blood, and even worse, he seems to have lost the will to survive. I found him lying over there on the ground. He didn't even resist when I removed the bullet from his shoulder and seared the wound to stop the bleeding. I can't get him back on his feet to reach the ranch. An infection will spread through his body if the wound is not treated. I doubt he will live through the night. I fear only Anna can save him, but we are still miles from the ranch. Time is not on our side."

Babcock Ranch

Chapter 14

Anna tried to keep her mind focused on the rugged path, but David's remark about Jake's feelings for her distracted her. Do I love him? What is love supposed to feel like? I've never been in love, but I have never felt the way I feel when he is near me. He excites me. I can hardly wait to see him every night at supper even though he annoys me, and we end up bickering. I try extra hard to please him, and I couldn't bear it if something happened to him. I can't imagine my life without him in it. She shivered. I do love him. Her horse slipped on loose stones, and she almost fell off. Her thoughts about love immediately vanished. If she wanted to live to see Jake again, she had to concentrate on climbing the treacherous trek to the southern passage alive.

Her horse was unfamiliar with the mountain trail, and she continuously had to encourage him to move forward. Several times the young gelding refused to ascend a steep and narrow incline, and she had to dismount to pull him. She had only ridden him once

Babcock Ranch

before—the first day she had arrived. She regretted now she hadn't done more riding and spent more time with him so he would have more trust in her.

Maximus led the way. He easily leaped across narrow crevices and clawed his way up steep slopes. He frequently looked back to make sure she was following him.

David was struggling with his horse, too. "Miss Babcock, are you sure you want to continue? Our horses are skittish about the narrowness of the passageways and the steepness of the inclines. Horses instinctively don't like tight places or loose footing."

Anna shook her head. "You can turn back, David. I will understand, but I know that Jake and Avonaco are out here because of me. The stallion is badly hurt or else he would have come to the ranch on his own."

David rode up beside her. "I don't understand. Why would the stallion come to the ranch?"

"Because it's a full moon, and he belongs to me." She could see the confusion in David's eyes. "It's a long story. We are almost to the

Babcock Ranch

summit, and the path will be easier once we reach it, but you can turn around now if you want. The three most important beings in the world to me are up there somewhere. I won't quit climbing until I find them."

David said nothing and continued to follow her lead.

Once they reached the wider passage, Anna urged her horse to keep up with Maximus. David fell behind, but she couldn't waste time slowing down to let him catch up. Maximus began running faster and faster, and she knew he could sense that Luna was near. She urged her horse into a gallop. Ahead she saw dark silhouettes of other riders. Her heart raced as she realized it was not Avonaco and Jake. It was too late for her to seek cover or to warn David. The riders had already seen her. One of the men raised his rifle and fired a shot. Her horse reared and slid on the loose stones toward a deep drop off. She jumped to the ground and clung tightly to the reins, pulling with all her strength until the horse finally regained his footing. The poor animal shook and snorted. She leaned against him and ran her hand down his neck. "You're all right fellow."

Babcock Ranch

She whirled around and glared at the unshaven, rough-looking riders. "You almost made us fall over the cliff."

Tom Jacobs jumped down from his horse and aimed his gun at her. "Now just what would a lovely lady like yourself be doing up here in the mountains at night."

Anna tried to appear calm, but inside she was trembling more than her horse. She knew the three riders were Holloway's men. The same men who had shot Luna. She inhaled a deep breath and stared back at the menacing man. "I could ask you the same thing. Why are you up here at this time of night? Hunting for wolves?" Jacobs sneered.

Anna started to get back on her horse, but he grabbed her arm and whirled her around.

From a large rock above her, Maximus lunged through the air and landed on top of Jacobs. The gun fell to the ground, and Anna quickly grabbed it. Behind the other two riders, David stepped out from the darkness. "Move, and I'll blow you off your horses."

Babcock Ranch

Maximus clawed at Jacobs' shirt and bit his neck. Jacobs writhed around on the ground, covering his face with his arms. "Call your dog off, for god's sake."

Anna held the gun next to Jacob's head. "Come, Maximus." Maximus slowly backed away from Jacobs but continued to growl ferociously. He bared his teeth, and his hackles stood high on his neck. He crouched low, ready to pounce if Jacobs moved.

David removed the guns from the saddle holsters of the two other men and tossed them over the side of the mountain. "Get down slowly and keep your hands where I can see them." He unwound the rope from each of their saddles and used it to tie their hands and feet.

Anna continued to hold the gun against Jacobs' head. He tried to sit up, but Maximus pounced on him and laid across his chest staring into his eyes. "Get this wild dog off me. We didn't mean any harm."

Anna pushed the gun harder against his head. "You shot my horse."

"Your horse? If you mean that wild stallion, he's a horse thief. That's how we treat horse thieves out here."

Babcock Ranch

David reached down and yanked him up from the ground. He tied his hands behind his back and dragged him over to where he had tied the other two men back to back. Anna called for Maximus. "I'm going to ride on ahead, David. I think it's best if you stay here to make sure these idiots don't get loose and to keep the wolves from eating them. When I find Jake and Avonaco, I will send one of them back to help you take them down the mountain."

Maximus ran ahead of her. After several miles, he ran even faster yipping and barking. Luna was near.

In the moonlight, Anna saw another rider racing toward her. She recognized Jake. When he reached her, he catapulted to the ground and pulled her down from her horse into his arms. He held her so tight that she struggled to breathe. He finally loosened his hold on her and stepped back to look into her eyes. "We heard a gunshot. I was afraid it might have been the Holloways. I knew you would try to find us and feared they were shooting at you."

"Have you found Luna?"

Babcock Ranch

Jake pulled her back into his arms and held her tight. He whispered through her hair. "It's not good, Anna. He's been shot and has lost a lot of blood. Avonaco fears he won't make it through the night."

She pushed away from him. "Take me to him, Jake. Now!"

She followed Jake as they galloped along the moonlit path. When they reached the campsite, she jumped from her horse and ran to Luna. Maximus was laying next to the giant horse lightly licking his muzzle. Anna knelt beside them. She gently stroked Luna's giant neck and ran her fingers through his silky mane. She leaned in close to him and whispered in his ear.

For the first time since Avonaco had found him, the giant horse opened his eyes and struggled to lift his head, but he immediately let it fall to the ground and once more closed his eyes. Anna leaned over him and rubbed his giant jowl. Tears streamed down her face and fell onto his neck. "Please, Luna. Get up, please." She gently shook him, but he didn't respond.

Avonaco knelt beside her. "He is weak Archisa. Did you bring anything that could fight the infection?"

Babcock Ranch

"In my saddle bag. I brought the first-aid kit. There is powder in there that Granny always used."

Jake rushed to her horse and returned with the first-aid kit. Avonaco immediately sprinkled the powder into the wound. He squeezed her hand. "Now it is up to the Great Father in the sky and Luna."

"I know, Avonaco. I know." Anna leaned closer to Luna's ear.

"Fight, Luna. Fight like you did years ago the day you were born. We have many more dances in the moonlight. You can't leave me. You are part of my soul. Please, please Luna, fight." She laid her head on his withers and sobbed. Jake covered her with a blanket and sat down next to her. He gently brushed her hair away from her wet face and bent over to kiss the top of her head.

For a long time, no one spoke. Jake fell asleep next to her. Suddenly Anna sat up. "Oh my gosh. David!" She gently shook Jake, and he jumped up from the ground. He staggered and turned around in circles. For a moment she feared he might step on her. "Jake, wake up."

Babcock Ranch

He shook his head and opened his eyes wide. "What is it? I'm sorry. I must have fallen asleep."

"I didn't mean to startle you, but I forgot to tell you that David is holding the three Holloway men captive about two miles from here. We ran into them on the way. The gunshot you heard was from them, but with the help of Maximus and David, they are currently tied up. David is waiting for one of you to help him take them down the mountain."

Avonaco jumped up and headed toward the horses. "I will go, Jake. You stay here with Anna."

Jake stared at her and sat back down next to her. "Will you never cease to amaze me?"

Anna patted Maximus on the head. "David and I had a lot of help capturing them."

Luna suddenly lunged forward and with tremendous effort and encouragement from the barking Maximus, he scrambled to his feet. Jake backed quickly away from the giant horse. His size and massive body intimidated him, but not Anna. She ducked under Luna's

Babcock Ranch

massive head and spread her arms across his broad chest. "I knew you wouldn't leave me to dance alone in the moonlight."

Babcock Ranch

Chapter 15

For the next two weeks, Anna and Maximus slept in the barn to be near Luna. Dr. Canfield gathered his equipment after checking on him for the second time since she had brought him home. "You know, Anna, if you hadn't used your grandmother's homemade antiseptic powder, Luna would have died of infection. You don't happen to know what she put into the powder, do you? She used to make some for me, but she would never tell me what she put in it. I use it all the time for every animal I treat, and I'm running out of it." As they left the barn, Anna linked her arm with his. "I am learning that I should have paid more attention to a lot of things Granny did. I have seen her make the powder dozens of times, but I never saw her refer to a written formula. I will look around for it, but if the recipe for the powder is anything like her cooking recipes, she never wrote anything down but the list of ingredients without proportions or any other useful information." She sighed and glanced toward the sky. "It's a shame we never take time to ask questions or pay attention to

Babcock Ranch

loved ones while they're with us. We go through life assuming they will always be here. I would give anything for one more day with her. I have so many things I want to tell and ask her. I miss her every day."

Dr. Canfield patted her hand, "We all miss her around here. There aren't many of us that she didn't help out at one time or another. Billings is so different now. It's become just another railroad town without the heart and closeness we had before."

"I think Granny felt the same way."

Dr. Canfield nodded. "I know she did. We used to complain about it every time we saw each other. Well, I've got to get going. Let me know if you find the powder recipe." He climbed into his carriage and looked down at her. "I don't think there's any reason for me to check on Luna again. He's in good physical health, but I can't say the same for his mental state. He's despondent. That's why he's not eating. You need to decide when to turn him loose, Anna. I know he was born on this ranch, and you think you are protecting him by keeping him here, but he will die soon unless you let him go. He's

Babcock Ranch

wild, and he needs to be set free." He looked up at the southern passage. "Somewhere up there is a band of mares and young fillies and colts searching for him, and he knows it."

Tears filled her eyes. "I know, but I'm worried he'll just end up getting shot again."

"Perhaps, but his chances of living are better up there than down here. Think about it."

After he left, Anna led Luna into the small paddock. "Maybe if you get some sun you will feel better." She turned him loose, and he jumped and kicked his hind legs high into the air for several minutes. He shook his body and tossed his head from side-to-side. She watched him closely as he paced back and forth staring at the mountain. Suddenly, he reared and blasted a mournful whinny. She knew he was calling to his harem. When she was much younger, she had learned the ways of wild horses from Avonaco. He had told her that mares and stallions play different roles in the family group. A dominant mare assumes responsibility for leading the group to food, water, and shelter from storms. The stallion plays the role of

Babcock Ranch

protector and follows at the rear of the band whenever they are on the move and positions himself outside of the group when they are grazing—always alert to any threat to the others. The bond between the band is strong, and they stay together all day every day unless something or someone interferes. She looked out in the distance at the mountain and sighed. "I am that someone who is interfering with his family."

Luna trotted over to where she was sitting on the rail fence. He rested his giant head on her knee. She took his thick, coarse forelock in her hand and gently ran her fingers through it to remove the tangles. "I know. You want to go home, don't you? Soon, my friend, I promise."

After supper that night, Anna told Avonaco what Dr. Canfield had said to her.

Avonaco took her hand in his. "Dr. Canfield is right. Luna belongs with his harem. He won't survive here without them. He is grieving, and just as you are missing your grandmother and Jake since he moved into town, Luna is missing his family. He knows they are out

Babcock Ranch

there wanting him and waiting for his return, but unlike you, he is not free to go to them. You can ride into town to see Jake anytime you want, but Luna doesn't have that freedom. You must set him free again, Archisa, or he will grieve himself to death. You are selfish to keep him here. You aren't protecting him; you are killing him."

"I know; I know, but in her letter, Granny said I should bring him home to protect and care for him. I think I know a way to do that without having to keep him separated from his harem. To make it happen though, I will need the help of you and the other ranch hands. Will you help me?"

Babcock Ranch

Chapter 16

Jake leaned against the side of the Grand Hotel. It was dusk, and he knew Morse's clerk, Henry Slater, would soon be walking toward the boarding house near the hotel. Jake had watched him walk by the hotel every night. He glanced down the street and spotted Henry. When he was closer, Jake stepped out of the shadows in front of him.

Henry jumped back and threw his hands up in the air. "I don't have anything worth stealing."

Jake chuckled. "Are you always so nervous? You can put your hands down. I just want to ask you a few questions."

Henry adjusted his glasses and squinted to see more clearly in the dim light. He leaned in close to Jake. "I recognize you. You're that man who came into the office with Anna Babcock a few weeks ago." He stepped around Jake and hurried down the boardwalk.

Jake whirled around and chased after him. "Wait, Henry. All I want is to ask you a few questions."

Babcock Ranch

Henry increased his pace.

When he caught up with him, Jake grabbed his shoulder and spun him around. "Why are you so afraid to talk with me?"

Henry jerked away. "Please, leave me alone. I know nothing about the Babcock Ranch tax payment." Henry tried to brush past him again.

Jake stepped in front of him to block his escape. "What makes you think I am going to ask you about Mrs. Babcock's tax payment?"

"Well, weren't you? I wasn't born in the woods, Mr. Crowley."

"So, you know my name, do you? I don't recall identifying myself when we first met."

Henry stepped sideways, but Jake again blocked his way. "You know, Henry, we could continue this dance back and forth for hours, or you can agree to come back to the hotel with me, and I will treat you to a nice meal."

Henry's whole body slumped. "Please, Mr. Crowley, give me leave. I can't be seen with you or.." He looked behind him to see if there was anyone else in the street.

Babcock Ranch

"Or what, Henry? Has someone threatened you?"

Henry straightened his posture. "Let me just say, Mr. Crowley, that I like my job, and I value my life. To be seen talking to you could end both."

Jake gently placed his hand on Henry's shoulder. "You're a smart man Henry. Surely you know that the best protection is for you to help me put Morse and Holloway behind bars. Think about it. I already have gone over the books, and I know they don't balance. What I need to prove is that Morse is responsible for the discrepancy, not you."

Henry's eyes widened. "Me? I have not done anything wrong, Mr. Crowley. I know there are missing funds, but I certainly didn't take any money."

Jake patted him on the shoulder. "According to Morse you did, and let me remind you that his word will carry more weight in court than yours. Think about it, Henry."

He stepped aside, and Henry scurried away.

Babcock Ranch

Jake stared after him, then slowly headed back to the hotel for another meal alone. He wondered what Anna fixed for supper tonight. Though he hated to admit it, she was an excellent cook. In fact, she was good at everything she did. "God, I miss her."

Colonel Holloway was outside the hotel leaning against the wall and smoking a cigar when Jake approached. "Mr. Crowley, it's nice to see you."

Jake frowned. "I bet it is."

Colonel Holloway chuckled. "There's no need for us to be on opposite sides of this Babcock mess."

Jake tipped his hat back. "What Babcock mess are you talking about, Colonel?" He observed the Colonel carefully, but Holloway remained stone-faced.

"Come now, Crowley. Billings is still a relatively small town, and news travels fast around here. In case you missed it, your filings were listed in the Gazette last week. I wasn't as surprised as some of the other locals to discover you were a lawyer."

Jake shifted his weight. "And why is that, Holloway?"

Babcock Ranch

"Simple really. I had the Pinkerton Detective Agency run a check on you when you first arrived out here. I'm a businessman and a gambler, Mr. Crowley, and I make it a habit to check out people I don't think fit the façade they hide behind. I knew you weren't the typical ranch hand the first time I saw you."

Jake removed his hat and flipped it around in his hand. "Do you want something, Holloway? If not, you'll have to excuse me. I'm hungry, and I have some preparation to finish for the hearing next week."

Holloway pushed away from the wall. "I do want something, Crowley."

Jake shook his head. "And what could you possibly want from me."

"Two things, actually. I want you to put Morse behind bars where he belongs. Dishonesty does not belong in government affairs."

Jake sneered. "Does that mean you have decided not to run for State Senator?"

Babcock Ranch

Holloway ignored him. "The second thing I want is for you to drop the injunction to keep the Babcock property from being auctioned off."

Jake laughed. "I intend to grant your first wish, but as for your second—not a chance, Holloway."

"I intend to own that land, Crowley. If I can't get it through the auction, I will buy it directly from Anna Babcock."

Jake smiled. "She wouldn't sell it to you if you were the last man on earth."

Colonel Holloway shrugged. "I wouldn't be too sure of that, Jake. I understand she wants to return to New York. I am in a position to make her an offer that would let her do just that and have a nice nest egg to live comfortably and pursue her art. I figure she'll have trouble walking away from such a chance."

Jake shoved him aside and entered the hotel.

Babcock Ranch

Chapter 17

Anna and the ranch hands were up before dawn. She mounted her horse, and she and Maximus ponied Luna out of the barn toward the open pasture. Luna's ears were pitched forward as far as they could go, and he pulled hard against the lead rope. He could sense she was going to set him free. When they reached the edge of the southern passage, Anna jumped down from her horse and pulled Luna's giant head down to stare into his eyes. "Go find them, Luna." He gently bumped against her and pawed at the ground. When she removed the halter from around his neck, he sped away with his tail in the air and his mane flying in the wind.

Maximus circled her feet, yipping, and whining. Anna knelt and patted him. "Follow him, Maximus." As she knew he would, he shot across the pasture in pursuit of Luna. She quickly mounted her horse, and Avonaco and the others galloped out to join her. Avonaco rode up beside her. "Let's go. We can't let them get too far ahead of us, or we will lose them."

Babcock Ranch

The ride up the mountain was less treacherous in the daylight, but they were not as quick as the two animals, and Anna feared they had lost their trail. When they came to a place where another passage crossed theirs, Avonaco jumped down from his horse and carefully examined the ground. He motioned for them to take the other passage leading to a canyon below them. The descending passage was steep, and their horses struggled to keep from sliding on the loose stones.

Anna heard Israel grumbling to David. "Man sakes, this is crazy. We are risking our lives to find a wild horse we just turned loose. Most ranchers want the animal dead anyway. I don't get it?" David didn't respond to him.

When they finally reached the level ground of the canyon, Avonaco pulled up his horse and stared at the herd of cattle in front of them. David rode up beside him. "Well, I'll be. My bet is those are our missing heads. I'll go check the brand." He rode into the open pasture before Avonaco could stop him.

Babcock Ranch

A shot rang out, and they watched in horror as David fell from his horse. Avonaco jumped to the ground. He ran to Anna and snatched her down from her horse dragging her behind a huge boulder. "Stay put, Anna. Don't move from this spot until you hear from me." Robert and Israel jumped from their horses, and, with guns drawn, they made their way behind the rocks toward the direction of the gunshots.

Anna looked up at Avonaco with tear-filled eyes. "This is all my fault. I should have just let Luna go."

Avonaco shook his head. "It won't help now to worry about blame. Stay here. Don't move until you hear my whistle, or I come back to get you."

Anna sank to the ground as she watched him climb higher among the rocks. Time seemed to stand still. She strained to listen for his whistle, but she heard only the bawling of the cattle and the high-pitched scream of a red-tailed hawk circling above her. Suddenly, a firestorm of shots echoed across the canyon, and she covered her ears. Tears streamed down her face. A long eerie silence followed.

Babcock Ranch

Impatient to see what was happening, she crept out of her hiding place. A bullet buzzed past her and ricocheted off a nearby rock causing her to dive back behind the boulder. Another rapid series of shots erupted. She crouched closer to the rock and prayed. Pulling her knees tight against her chest, she tried to make herself as small as possible. Her heart raced, and she trembled and shivered even though her body felt like it was on fire.

As quickly as it had started the gunfire ceased. After minutes that seemed like hours, she recognized the whistle from Avonaco. She cautiously crept from behind the rock. In the open pasture, she saw Israel lifting David from the ground and resting his head in his lap. She jumped on her horse and sped across the pasture.

When she reached him, Israel looked up at her with tear-filled eyes. "He's bleeding pretty bad. The bullet just missed his chest and hit his shoulder. Luckily the fall from the horse must have knocked him out. If he had moved, they would have riddled his body with gunshot."

Babcock Ranch

Anna looked around for Avonaco and Robert. "Where are the others, Israel?"

"They're busy attending to the Holloway men."

Anna tore David's shirt away from the wound. "It looks like the bullet went straight through the muscle."

Israel turned David slightly and looked at his back. "Sure, enough. There's an exit hole behind his shoulder blade."

Anna ran to her horse and grabbed the first aid kit. She poured the last of her grandmother's powder over David's wound and held a piece of cloth against it to stop the bleeding.

Israel jerked off his shirt and tore a strip of it from around the bottom to wrap around David's shoulder and back. "This will have to do for pressure Miss Babcock, until we get him back to the ranch."

David moaned and blinked several times. He reached toward his shoulder, and Anna grabbed his hand. "Don't touch the bandage, David."

He slowly moved his head back and forth. "What the hell happened?"

Babcock Ranch

Israel helped him sit up. "You got shot, buddy. Stay here with Miss Babcock. I'll go get the horses. Do you think you can ride?"

David tried to stand up but immediately dropped to the ground. "The world is spinning around like crazy."

Anna reached out to steady him. "You hit your head when you fell off your horse. I don't think you should try to ride on your own. The passage back to the ranch is pretty steep."

Israel stood and looked around. "There has to be another path out of this canyon. There's no way the Holloways could have driven our cattle over the mountain passage."

In the distance, Anna spotted Avonaco and Robert approaching them. She stared in horror when she saw the bodies of two men draped across the back of their horses. Tom Jacobs' hands were tied to the saddle horn, and Robert was towing his horse.

Avonaco knelt beside David. "Thank goodness you're alive. I should have warned you that Holloway's men were out on bail. The trespassing charge was not strong enough to hold them."

Babcock Ranch

David flashed a weak smile. "You'd think I'd have known better than to ride into the open toward a herd of stolen cattle. I should have known there'd be someone guarding them."

Avonaco picked up David's hat lying on the ground next to him and plopped it on David's head. "Come on, let's get you back to the ranch. You can ride on my horse in front of me."

Israel helped Avonaco lift David onto his horse. He then turned to glare at Jacobs. "How the hell did you get these cattle in here?"

Jacobs snarled. "I'd bet you'd like to know that wouldn't you?"

Robert turned around in his saddle and aimed his gun at Jacobs. "You've got three seconds to tell us, or you'll be riding back to town in the same position as your buddies." He cocked the hammer on his Colt pistol. "One, two…"

"OK, OK. I'll tell you." Jacobs pointed toward a narrow exit out of the canyon. "Through there. Straight ahead about 10 miles the public lands butt up against the back pasture of the Babcock Ranch."

Robert slowly released the hammer of his gun. "You'd better be right."

Babcock Ranch

Avonaco looked over at Anna. "I'm going ahead with Israel. "Do you think you can help Robert drive the cattle behind us?"

Anna feigned a look of confidence. "Of course, I can." It had been years since she had ridden on a cattle drive, and she silently prayed she'd remember what to do.

Avonaco detected her uncertainty. "You can do this, Anna. You used to move cattle with us all the time. It will come back to you." He glanced up at the mountain. "I'm sorry about Luna, but I'm certain you understand why we must head back."

"I know, Avonaco. It was a silly plan anyway. I should just let nature follow its course." She quickly turned her horse around to hide the tears gathering in her eyes.

Babcock Ranch

Chapter 18

When Jake heard about the shooting, he immediately rode out to the ranch. Anna looked up from mucking out one of the stalls when he charged into the barn. He grabbed her into his arms before she could utter a word. "Thank God, you weren't hurt." He held her close for several minutes rocking her back and forth until finally stepping away from her. He stared into her startled eyes. "Whatever possessed you to drag everyone on the ranch up that mountain on such a dangerous trek to recapture a horse you set loose?"

Anna pulled away from him. "Don't scold me like a child, Jake. I didn't mean for it to end the way it did. Don't you understand that?"

Jake grabbed her hand. "What I understand is that you almost got David killed. Don't you realize that if all of you had ridden into that open pasture with him, you could all have been shot? And for what? To deny a wild horse his freedom?"

Anna yanked her hand away from him. "I want to protect Luna, Jake. You know that."

Babcock Ranch

"When will you learn he doesn't need or want to be protected. You risked the lives of everyone on this ranch for a selfish desire to keep him fenced in for the rest of his life."

Anna threw down the rake and stormed out of the barn. Jake chased after her and swung her around. "I'm sorry. I didn't mean to call you selfish. I know you want to protect him but look at what has happened. The ranch is short-handed now with both David and me unable to help the others. What's even worse, they may all be arrested because Holloway has accused them of murder."

Anna's eyes opened wide. "Murder? His men were shooting at us. They stole our cattle, for god's sake."

Jake shook his head. "Jacobs claims Avonaco and the others ambushed them and that the cattle in the canyon were loose on public lands. He says his men didn't recognize the Babcock brand. I convinced the Sheriff to hold off arresting the ranch hands until after the Morse trial. Thank God he knows Jacobs is a low-life liar, but he won't be able to avoid coming after them for very long. If I can't convict Holloway on fraud along with Morse, and Jacobs refuses to tell the truth, Holloway will insist the Sheriff lock up all four of them until they get a hearing. Then what? The two of us can't herd 2500 head of cattle by ourselves, for god's sakes. It could be weeks before they get a hearing and even then, it will be their word against Jacobs. Avonaco will be suspect because he is Cheyenne. Holloway will try to blame him for the whole mess."

Anna lowered her head and kicked at the dirt. "People out here are uncivilized ruffians, and you have become one of them. I don't belong here anymore. I wish I could get on the next train heading back to civilization."

Jake leaned in close to her. "Right. Just go ahead and leave us so-called ruffians to clean up the messes you created. Maybe you *should* go back to New York. You certainly have upset the peace I used to enjoy out here." He was sorry the moment the angry words left his mouth. He reached for her hand, but she stepped away from him. The pain shining in her eyes choked him. "I didn't mean that, Anna. You know I didn't. Sometimes you just drive me nuts."

Babcock Ranch

She whirled around and ran into the house. He heard the bolt slam into the lock on the door. Yanking his hat off, he hurled it to the ground. "Anna, for god's sake come out here and talk to me. I didn't mean what I said." He inhaled a long, deep breath. "I love you, Anna, and I want you here with me forever. Don't you know that by now?" He waited for a response, but none came. "OK, fine. Have it your way. You certainly have your grandmother's stubbornness; there's no denying that."

He grabbed his hat and stormed off the porch. He had to return to town. Henry Slater, his only witness aside from Anna, had mysteriously disappeared.

Babcock Ranch

Chapter 19

Anna ran from her bedroom into the kitchen. She struggled with the lock on the door and finally burst out onto the porch. She stared at the cloud of dust in the distance and threw up her hands. "What is wrong with me? I can't do anything right. I've ruined everything." She brushed a tear from her cheek. "Of all the good qualities of my grandmother, why did I inherit only her stubbornness?" She turned around to go back inside and headed toward her grandmother's parlor. When life overwhelmed her, she could always find comfort in her art.

Lifting the cover from the painting she had started weeks ago, she stared at the peaceful scene and tried to recapture the inspiration she had felt the day she created it. Tears blurred her vision, and the colors seemed to run together on the canvas. The enchantment of the scene was now so far removed from her reality that it irritated rather than inspired her. She yanked the cloth back over it and walked over to the window. She had never felt so alone—even more so today

Babcock Ranch

than on the first day she had arrived in New York. There she had been surrounded by people—granted most of them were strangers, but someone was always nearby. She stared at the mountain. "Where are you Luna and Maximus? I need you."

She turned away from the window and picked up the afghan draped across the back of her grandmother's rocker. She wrapped it tightly around her—not for the warmth it provided but for the comfort it gave her. "Oh, Granny, I have made such a mess of everything."

A knock on the door startled her. "Maybe Jake has come back." She hurried into the kitchen and looked out the window. A horse slathered in sweat breathed heavily near the edge of the porch, but it wasn't Jake's horse. She raised on her tiptoes and leaned closer to the window trying to see who had knocked on the door, but the person was facing away from her. It was a man, but she couldn't tell who he was. She sank to the floor hoping he hadn't seen her through the window. She glanced over at the door and was relieved to see she had locked it.

Babcock Ranch

Staying low, she hurried to the gun cabinet in the dining room. Grabbing a shotgun and shells from the wooden case, she broke open the gun's barrel, and with shaking hands, she managed to drop the shells into the chamber and snap the gun closed. The person knocked again—this time louder.

Her hands were cold and damp and her breathing quick and shallow. She hadn't shot a gun in years and prayed she could fire it if necessary. She stared at the door trying to decide whether she should open it.

Another loud knock jarred her out of her stupor. It sounded as if the person was desperately pounding on the door with both hands.

She tightened her grip on the gun. "Who is it?"

"It's Henry Slater. Please let me in. I need to speak to Jake Crowley."

Anna tried to recall the name, but it was unfamiliar. "Should I know you?"

"Miss Babcock, please let me in. I am Mr. Morse's clerk."

Babcock Ranch

She quickly laid the gun down on the dining room table and hurried to unlock the door.

Henry burst into the kitchen and slammed the door behind him. He leaned against it and slowly slid to the floor.

Anna stared at the distraught, pale-faced man. Fear poured from his eyes. He was trembling, and his lips were colorless.

"Good grief, Mr. Slater. Is someone chasing you? You look as if you might faint."

Henry muttered something but Anna couldn't understand him. She hurried to the stove and threw a few pieces of wood into the firebox.

"I'll fix you some hot tea. Perhaps, that will make you feel better. I'm sorry I don't have anything stronger to offer you. My grandmother never allowed liquor on the ranch."

She glanced at him. He hadn't moved. His chin rested on his chest, and his eyes were closed. She went over to him and knelt beside him. "Mr. Slater, are you sick or injured?"

Babcock Ranch

He raised his head and looked at her with glazed eyes. His lips quivered, and his voice was barely audible. "I haven't slept or eaten in two days—been hiding in the mountains."

Anna tucked her arm under his shoulder. "Let me help you get up and over to the table. I'll heat some stew from last night. Once you get food into you, you'll feel better, and you can tell me why you were hiding in the mountains."

Henry shook his head. "If you don't mind, I'll just sit here a while longer. I don't think I can stand just yet."

Anna finished making the tea and warming the stew. "Henry, I'm sorry, but Jake isn't here. He's been staying in town. Unfortunately, I don't know when or if he'll be back before the trial. I assume your hiding in the mountains has something to do with our case against Morse, right?

Henry struggled to stand and stumbled over to the table. Anna ran to support him. "My goodness, you are as weak as a kitten." Once she helped him into a chair, she hurried to the stove and brought him the stew and tea. "Here eat this, and then we'll talk."

Babcock Ranch

When Henry picked up the cup, his hands trembled, and Anna quickly grabbed it to keep him from dumping the tea. "Here let me help you. Are you shaking because you are cold or are you frightened?"

Henry looked at her for the first time. "I can't go into town, Miss Babcock."

Anna could see the fear in his eyes. "Why is that Henry?"

Henry took another gulp of the tea. "I'm a wanted man, Miss Babcock. Mr. Crowley warned me, but I thought he was bluffing to get me to talk to him."

"Jake never bluffs, Henry. But I can't fathom that you did anything so horrible to make you a wanted man. You were so shy and helpful that day in the Treasurer's Office that I find it hard to believe you would commit a crime."

Henry managed a half smile. "That's just it, Miss Babcock. I haven't done anything wrong. I have followed the ten commandments without exception since I was old enough to understand what they meant. I swear it."

Babcock Ranch

Anna patted his hand. "I believe you, Henry. Who accused you of wrongdoing? Surely, it wasn't Jake. He would never falsely accuse anyone."

Henry shook his head. "No, it wasn't Mr. Crowley. I should have listened to him when he warned me that Mr. Morse was trying to pin the lost money from your grandmother's payment on me."

Anna sat up straighter. "So, you know she paid her taxes."

"No, Miss Babcock, I can't help you there. If she paid them, she must have come in after I left the office and made her payment. I never saw her, a receipt or any money."

Anna jumped up from her chair. "I'll be right back, Henry. Eat some more of the stew." She hurried into her grandmother's parlor and opened the hidden panel in her desk. She pulled out the tax receipt. As she closed the small door, she noticed a piece of paper she hadn't seen before. Reaching inside the small compartment, she picked up the note. "Well, I'll be. The formula for the powder, complete with proportions and instructions for making it. This is going to please Dr. Canfield."

Babcock Ranch

When she returned to the kitchen, Henry was asleep with his head resting on the table. She gently shook him.

He jumped up, knocking over the chair and holding his hands in the air.

"Easy, Henry. I didn't mean to startle you. I'm sorry. You are certainly overwrought."

"I thought you were the Sheriff. I'm a little jumpy, I guess."

Anna chuckled. "A little? I have something to show you, but you have to promise me you aren't here under the pretense to help Mr. Morse."

Henry frowned. "Why would I help him? He's the reason I had to leave town in the first place."

"OK. I guess I can trust you." She carefully unfolded the receipt and held it up for him to see.

When he reached for it, she quickly withdrew it behind her back. "I don't want you to touch it, Henry. Just look at it and tell me if it is your handwriting."

Babcock Ranch

"Hold it closer, then. Somewhere in the mountains, I lost my glasses."

"As long as you don't try to grab it, I'll hold it closer."

Henry squinted and carefully studied the receipt. "No, that's Mr. Morse's handwriting, not mine. So, your grandmother did pay her taxes. That must be why he had me recopy the ledger page and add your grandmother's name to it." He wrinkled his brow. "That helps you, but it doesn't do me any good. If anything, it makes me more vulnerable. It doesn't prove I didn't steal the money."

Anna folded up the receipt. "Henry, why don't you come with me. I'll take you to the bunkhouse, and you can get some rest there. The ranch hands won't be back for several hours. You can join us for dinner, and maybe they can help us figure out how to help you." She laid her hand on his shoulder. "I am afraid I can't think of anything right now that will free you from blame unless Jake somehow proves that Morse stole the money or gets Morse to admit that he stole it."

Henry slumped. "I think we both know that's not likely to happen. I may as well turn myself in. I'm as much as convicted already."

Babcock Ranch

Anna took his hand and squeezed it. "I wouldn't give up on Jake if I were you."

Babcock Ranch

Chapter 20

Jake arrived back in town tired and frustrated. He had messed everything up with Anna, and as of yet, he hadn't found Henry Slater. To make matters worse, he had no evidence that linked Morse to the missing money. He was confident he could prove that Anna's grandmother paid her taxes, but that was all he could do. What he really wanted was to free Henry from the blame of the missing money and prove that it was Morse and possibly Holloway who had stolen it.

He rubbed the back of his neck and rocked his head from side-to-side. Just the thought of Morse sent a streak of anger charging through him. When he had confronted Morse about the change to the ledger book he had spotted when he reviewed it, Morse had looked him straight in the eye and lied without flinching.

"We all must have simply missed Mrs. Babcock's entry when we looked at the ledger the day you were in my office. I actually am indebted to you for calling my attention to this whole mess. After

Babcock Ranch

you left that day, I looked at the ledger again and spotted Mrs.

Babcock's name right away. I then checked the deposits on that date

and for the following day. I noticed there was no listing of Mrs.

Babcock's payment. Since no one has access to the accounting

ledgers in my office other than myself and Henry, I knew right away

that he must have stolen the money."

Without Henry's testimony, Jake couldn't prove Morse had ordered

him to change the ledger. But even if Henry testified, it would be his

word against Morse, and as he had pointed out to Henry the other

night, Morse's word would carry more weight with the judge.

Jake pulled his horse up in front of the jail and slowly dismounted.

When he entered the outer office, Sheriff Jones looked up from his

desk. "Howdy, Jake. You look like you just lost your best friend.

What can I do for you?"

"I'm checking to see if you've found Henry Slater."

The Sheriff shook his head. "No, but to be honest, I haven't tried

very hard to find him. I don't believe Henry would do anything

dishonest. To keep Morse from breathing down my neck, I did send

Babcock Ranch

a deputy out to bring Henry in for questioning, but when the deputy confronted him, Henry gave him some excuse of needing something out of his room. The deputy waited outside of the boarding house for him instead of following Henry inside like he should have done. I guess he didn't think Henry would be brave enough to make a break for it. When Henry didn't come right back, my deputy broke into his room and discovered he was gone. He evidently jumped out the window. Lucky for him his room was on the first floor."

Jake shook his head. "He probably knew he didn't stand a chance against Morse. Did your deputy see which way he went?"

"No, he didn't, but according to the owner of the boarding house, he saw Henry riding out of town headed for the mountains. I haven't sent anyone to find him. I figure someone like Henry won't survive out there very long on his own. I suspect he'll come dragging back into town in a day or two unless the wolves get him."

Jake offered his hand to the Sheriff. "I am on the court docket for tomorrow. Let me know if you see him, will you?"

Babcock Ranch

"Sure thing. His sudden disappearance doesn't help his defense. Did you see the front page in yesterday's Gazette?"

Jake nodded. "They jumped on the story and already convicted him before he has had his day in court. Too bad. I kind of like old Henry, and I know he isn't guilty. Unfortunately, I can't prove it."

The Sheriff leaned in close to Jake and lowered his voice. "Holloway has been in here this morning insisting that I bring in your ranch hands for questioning. I don't know how much longer he will buy my excuses for not bringing them in."

Jake shuffled his feet. "I appreciate your help with that. Just give me a few more days. I'm still hoping for a miracle to drop from the sky, and then I can get Holloway and Morse out of your hair for a long time."

The sheriff rolled his eyes. "I hope your miracle comes through pretty quick. I can only hold Holloway off another day or two at the most."

Jake left the Sheriff Office and headed to the hotel. As he entered his room, he stepped on something lying on the floor. Looking down, he

Babcock Ranch

saw a small notebook. He tossed his hat and saddlebag onto the bed

and picked up the notepad. He carried it over to the window for more

light. The notes appeared to have been written by a female. The

handwriting was small and neat. He turned the pad over but didn't

see a name on it.

"Perhaps the lady who cleans my room dropped it."

He started to toss the notepad aside when the word Holloway

written on the first page caught his attention. He sat down on the

windowsill and skimmed the other pages. He read through the notes

a second and a third time. "This is my miracle."

He put the notepad in his saddlebag and headed toward the

mercantile. Now all I have to do is find out who wrote it. If anyone

can identify the handwriting, Courtney Livingston can. Practically

everyone in Billings has, at one time or another, signed for

something they purchased or ordered through the Mercantile or sent

a telegraph.

When he entered the Mercantile, he ducked behind a tall shelf to

avoid being seen by Colonel Holloway. Though he couldn't hear the

Babcock Ranch

conversation going on between Holloway and Courtney, he could tell by the look on Courtney's face she was angry and upset. Bright blotches of red covered her cheeks and neck, and tears filled her eyes.

He stepped out from behind the shelf. "What's going on, Courtney?" Holloway turned to face him. "This is none of your concern, Mr. Crowley. Now, if you'll excuse me, I have other business to attend to." Before exiting, he faced Courtney. "I will expect your payment by next Friday as per our contract."

Courtney didn't respond.

After Holloway left, Jake reached across the counter and took hold of her hand. "What was that all about Courtney?"

She pulled her hand loose and ran toward the back of the store behind the dressing screen. Jake followed her and could hear her sobbing.

"Stop crying, Courtney and come out here and tell me what's going on. I can't help you if I don't know what the problem is."

Babcock Ranch

After several minutes, Courtney shuffled from behind the screen. "I should have listened to Anna."

Jake frowned. "Anna? I don't understand."

"She warned me that Holloway might try to cheat me out of my business." She stomped her foot and threw up her hands. "Well, she was right. Holloway wants the balance due on my loan paid by next Friday, or he will foreclose. There is no way I can pay off the balance."

"He can't do that unless you signed an agreement that allows him to demand the full payment at any time during the term of the loan." Courtney slumped and looked away. "I didn't think he would actually do it."

Jake covered his eyes and let his hand slide slowly down his face, cupping his chin. "If you signed such an agreement, I doubt there is much you can do, but get me a copy of it, and I will see if I can find a loophole."

"Thank you, thank you." She threw her arms around his neck, then quickly stepped away from him. "By the way, why didn't you tell

Babcock Ranch

me you were a lawyer. I thought we were friends. Friends don't keep secrets."

Jake raised an eyebrow. "True friends also don't avoid one another."

Courtney flinched and looked away. "So, Anna told you?"

"No. Anna didn't say anything. You just haven't been around, and she was hesitant to stop in here when we were in town last time. I figured something was wrong."

"Tell her I'm sorry."

"For what?"

"She'll know."

"I don't deliver those kinds of messages. You need to tell her yourself. She's been having a rough time adjusting to the isolation and everything that's been going on. I imagine she would appreciate a friend right now."

Courtney drew in a deep breath. "I'll take care of it. Is she the reason you came in here? I take it you two have buried the hatchet and not in one another's heads."

Babcock Ranch

Jake smiled. "That's not exactly true, but I didn't come here on her behalf. Believe me; she can take care of herself. I need your help with something that could make the difference between allowing Holloway to intimidate and steal property from people like you or locking him up for a long time."

Courtney's eyes brightened. "I'm certainly willing to do anything to help with that. Anna knew immediately Holloway was a crook. I had forgotten what a good judge of character she was." She smiled. "Although, I bet she has changed her first opinion about you by now, right?"

Jake sighed. "I wouldn't be so sure of that. Anyway, back to why I came in here." He handed the notepad to Courtney. "Do you recognize the handwriting on these notes?"

She glanced at the notepad and quickly handed it back to him.

"That's Miss Collier's handwriting—Holloway's secretary. She always ends a sentence with a little circle instead of a period and the last stroke on her "m's" consistently dips below the line instead of connecting to the next letter."

Babcock Ranch

Jake chuckled. "You should work for the Pinkerton Detective Agency."

Courtney sighed. "I may have to if I can't figure out a way to pay off Holloway."

Chapter 21

Inside the courtroom the next day, Colonel Holloway glared at Miss Collier. "So, this is where you are. I expected you this morning at the office. What are you doing here?"

Miss Collier stared down at the linen handkerchief she was twisting around in her lap.

Jake interrupted. "I subpoenaed her, Colonel. Now, I suggest you sit down in the back of the courtroom."

Colonel Holloway leaned toward Jake. "I know what you are trying to do, Crawley. I assure you, you are wasting your time trying to connect me with any wrongdoing with the Babcock affair. Miss Collier knows very little if anything, about my business affairs. She has been a loyal employee since I first opened my office, and she will prove her loyalty to me today if she wants to keep her job. Did you know she supports her sick mother?" He laid his hand on Miss Collier's shoulder and squeezed it hard enough to cause her to sink into her chair and softly groan.

Babcock Ranch

Jake grabbed the Colonel's hand and pulled it off Miss Collier's shoulder. "I'm warning you, Colonel. Leave her alone."

Anna burst through the doors of the courtroom and rushed up to Jake. She grabbed him by the arm and pulled him away from the Colonel. "I'm sorry I'm late. I had a little trouble convincing Henry to come with me."

Jake frowned. "You have Henry with you? How did you find him?"

Anna shook her head. "Actually, he found me, but that's not important right now. What is important is that he's tied up under a blanket in the back of the wagon. Courtney is making sure he stays there until someone comes to get him." She reached up to gently close Jake's gaping mouth and smiled at him. "I discovered the skills of roping and tying up calves I learned in my early years are actually useful for other situations."

He took her hand. "Anna, I'm sorry about yesterday."

She raised on her tiptoes and lightly kissed his cheek. "I love you, too. We'll talk later. Right now, you need to concentrate on putting two crooks in jail where they belong."

Babcock Ranch

When the Sheriff led him into the courtroom, Jake met them and patted Henry on the back. "You are safe here, Henry. All you have to do is tell the truth. I'll do the rest."

Henry didn't look up or respond. Jake seated him in a chair next to Miss Collier. To Jake's surprise, she immediately grabbed Henry's hand and held on to it. "It's going to be all right, Henry. I gave Mr. Crawley my notepad."

Henry covered her hand with his and leaned in close to her. "I told you not to do that. It will put you in danger."

She smiled. "It was the right thing to do, Henry. We'll be all right."

Once the opening proceedings were completed, Jake called his first witness. "I would like to call the defendant, Mr. Samuel Morse to the stand, your honor.

Mr. Morse rose, and with his shoulders back, his chest out, and chin up high he strode confidently to the witness stand. After he was sworn in, he glanced at Judge Cooper. "I'll be glad to set this ridiculous situation straight, Judge. I know you are aware of the

Babcock Ranch

years I have honorably served the Office of Treasurer for the

County."

Jake cleared his throat. "Mr. Morse, the judge's opinion concerning

your past service is irrelevant. I would appreciate it if you would

simply answer the questions you are asked."

Mr. Morse sat up straighter in the chair and looked Jake straight in

the eyes with a smirk. "Of course, proceed Mr. Crowley."

Jake smiled. "Thank you, Mr. Morse. I intend to do just that, and for

your information, I don't need your permission to do so. Now that

we are clear as to who is in charge here, Mr. Morse, will you

describe what occurred in your office the day Miss Anna Babcock

and I visited you?"

Morse glared at him and briefly recounted the events, including the

lie they had simply missed locating Mrs. Babcock's name on the

payment list. He failed, however, to mention grabbing the receipt

from Anna and burning it.

"Mr. Morse is that all you care to tell the court of the events of that

day. Don't forget I was there, too."

Babcock Ranch

Morse squirmed. "That's all of any significance I can recall."

"You don't recall ripping a receipt for the payment of her grandmother's taxes from Miss Babcock's hand and burning it with the butt of your expensive cigar in your shiny, brass waste can?"

Morse's lawyer jumped up. "Objection. The prosecutor is leading the witness."

The judge pounded the gavel. "Sustained."

Jake nodded. "Sorry your honor, that was not my intention." He turned toward Morse. "After Miss Babcock and I left your office, what did you ask your clerk, Henry Slater, to do?"

Morse shrugged. "I don't recall asking Henry to do anything."

Henry jumped up and glared at Morse. "That's a lie, and you know it."

Miss Collier pulled him back into his seat. "You can't interrupt like that, Henry."

Judge Cooper pounded the gavel. "Young man, one more outburst from you, and I'll have the Sheriff haul you out of here and lock you up for contempt."

Babcock Ranch

Jake walked over to Henry. "Patience, Henry. You'll get your chance."

Henry slumped in his chair. "A lot of good it will do."

Jake continued by first calling Anna and then Henry to the stand. Each testified as to what had actually occurred on the day they had visited Morse's office.

Morse sneered at each of their testimonies. In an attempt to gain the sympathy of the judge, he shook his head and threw his hands up to show his affront at their accounts of the events. After each had testified, Morse leaned over to his lawyer and whispered just loud enough for the judge to hear. "Liars. That's what they are. Out and out liars."

Jake ignored him. "I would like to call my final witness to the stand. Miss Collier, will you please come forward.

Miss Collier stood up and walked briskly to the witness stand. Her air of confidence outshone that of Morse, but hers was not faked. Jake smiled at her grit.

Babcock Ranch

"Miss Collier, will you please tell the court about your association with Mr. Holloway and the defendant, Mr. Morse."

"Yes, Mr. Crawley. I have worked for Colonel Holloway for four years since he first opened his office. I am his private Secretary. I know Mr. Morse as a frequent visitor to Colonel Holloway's office."

Jake held up the notepad. "Do you recognize this?"

"Yes, sir. Of course, I do. It is mine. It is a record I made of a conversation between Mr. Morse and the Colonel on the day you and Miss Babcock had visited Mr. Morse's office."

Colonel Holloway jumped from his chair. His face was red and his eyes blazing with anger. "You wretched devil. How dare you eavesdrop on my conversations." He rushed up the aisle, pulling something from his pocket as he went. The sun pouring into the courtroom bounced off the shiny barrel of a small revolver. Jake threw himself in front of Miss Collier just as a shot rang out. Two deputies immediately tackled Holloway and pinned him to the ground. Henry leaped over the railing to help Miss Collier up, and

Babcock Ranch

Anna ran to Jake. Chaos erupted as Judge Cooper repeatedly pounded his gavel and called for order.

Anna helped Jake up from the floor. "You're bleeding, Jake. She tugged on the back of his suitcoat to remove it. "Let me look at the wound, Jake.

Jake tenderly grabbed hold of her hands to stop her. "It's just a scrape, Anna. I'm fine. The bullet just grazed my arm." He turned to Miss Collier. "Are you all right?"

Miss Collier straightened her hat and tugged on her jacket. "Just as I told you it would, the Colonel's temper got the best of him. I didn't expect the gunshot, though."

Jake glanced over at the defense table. The lawyer was crawling out from underneath the table, and Morse was gone.

Jake whirled around to face the judge. "Judge Cooper, where is Sam Morse?"

'How should I know, Mr. Crowley? I've never had such a chaotic scene as this in my courtroom, and believe me, I've heard a lot of

Babcock Ranch

nasty cases." He turned to the deputies holding Colonel Holloway. "Book him for attempted murder."

Holloway sneered. "I'll be out of jail before you take off your robe." Judge Cooper shook his head and peered down at him from the podium. "You forget, Mr. Holloway. I determine the cost of your bail, and I don't think you could possibly come up with the amount I have in mind." He pounded his gavel. "This court is adjourned pending the location of the defendant."

Henry took immediate charge of the manhunt for Morse. "I know exactly where he is. Follow me, but we had better hurry. He always has trouble with the combination on the safe. Most days I've had to open it for him. He's a pompous idiot. I never voted for him for Treasurer, but somehow he always got elected." Jake and the Sheriff followed Henry to the Treasurer's Office.

Henry pounded on the front door. "Come out with your hands up, Morse. The building is surrounded, and we know you are in there." Henry turned to the Sheriff. "I know I stole your thunder, Sheriff, but I have always dreamed of saying that."

Babcock Ranch

Sheriff Jones patted him on the back. "I couldn't have said it better, Henry."

The Sheriff pounded again on the door. "Morse, I'll give you to the count of ten to come out with your hands in the air before we crash through the doors with guns blazing." He counted slowly to ten, but Morse didn't appear.

Jake faced the Sheriff. "On your count?"

Henry shook his head. "No, wait. I'll go around to the back of the building and look through the window. If the drapes aren't drawn, I can see into his office."

Sheriff Jones grabbed Henry's arm. "Don't try to be a hero, Henry. Come back and tell us what you see, before you do anything."

"Yes, sir. Believe me; I am no hero."

After several minutes, Henry came back around to the front of the building. He was hunched over and holding his stomach. His face was colorless, and his eyes glazed.

Jake put his arm around his shoulders. "What is it, Henry? You look as if you have seen a ghost."

Babcock Ranch

Henry sank to the ground. "I did. He's not coming out. He's dead—

hung himself from his fancy chandelier."

Babcock Ranch

Chapter 23

Jake and Anna laid back on the cool grass and stared up at the beautiful, full moon. Holding hands, they quietly enjoyed the endless spray of stars, the fresh smell of alfalfa and bear-grass, and the night sounds of the prairie. The rich, low drone of bullfrogs, the bright, piercing chirp of crickets, and the smooth two-note hoot from a distant owl created a steady, rhythmic, symphony, interrupted on occasion only by the melancholic howl of a lonesome coyote.

The horror and trauma of the events of the past weeks were over. Colonel Holloway and Tom Jacobs would be eating their meals in the Deer Lodge prison for a long time. The territorial governor appointed Henry to serve out the remainder of Sam Morse's term as Treasurer, and Henry promptly hired his soon to be wife, Miss Collier, as his clerk. The Sheriff dropped the charges against Avonaco and the other ranch hands, and with Jake's help, Courtney refinanced her loan with the bank, and her threat of foreclosure vanished.

Babcock Ranch

After a long silence, Anna rolled over to look at Jake. "Though nighttime may be still, it is never silent. How much more pleasant are the sounds of the prairie than the noise of the hustle and bustle in New York."

Jake squeezed her hand. "I'm glad you have discovered that." He rose on one elbow and leaned over to gently kiss Anna's soft, warm lips.

Anna ran her finger gently down his cheek. In his eyes, she detected concern. "What is it, Jake? You look worried."

"Anna, do you think he will come if I am with you."

"He will come, and no doubt Maximus will come with him."

Jake tenderly ran his fingers through her soft hair that shimmered in the moonlight like long strands of black diamonds. "What if they don't come? Will you leave Babcock Ranch?"

She raised and kissed him on the cheek. "Oh Ye, of little faith. I know he is on his way." She rested her hand over her heart. "I can feel his closeness."

Babcock Ranch

Moments later, thunderous sounds of horse's hooves roared onto the prairie from the southern passage. Maximus charged across the pasture in front of a herd of beautiful horses.

Anna jumped up from the ground. "Luna has brought his family with him. We have both come home to stay." She threw both arms around Jake. "Even if he hadn't come, I would never have left you. Babcock Ranch is my home."

He pulled her into her arms and kissed her with a passion he had withheld since the first day they met. He slowly released her, and in a husky voice, he whispered, "Go, welcome him home."

Anna ran across the dew-covered grass to meet Luna and Maximus. Jake watched as her dance with Luna began—a spectacle that would always astonish him and intensify his everlasting love for her.

Quietly standing in the shadow of the bunkhouse, Avonaco raised his eyes to heaven. "Light shines again on Babcock Ranch. We are blessed by you once more, Ma heo'o, Creator of all physical and spiritual life."

Other Books by Author

Fiction

The Mansion

Breakfast with Friends

Raven's Call

Raven's Son

Raven's Rescue

Another Chance

Pennyworth Manor

Dear Friend

Non-Fiction

The Family Bitch

A Balanced Approach to Reading

Children's Books

Miss Molly Series

Dudley Dreads Decisions

Babcock Ranch